MW01502597

Karen—
Thank you for
supporting Seth on
his birthday.

D

PORTER

This is a work of fiction. Names, characters, places, and incidents either are the product of the author's imagination or are used fictitiously. Any resemblance to actual persons, living or dead, events or locales is entirely coincidental.

ISBN 978-1530249640

Acknowledgments

The usual suspects always come first where these things are concerned: My grandmother, my mom, and Lola. Without these three women, I wouldn't be where I am today. Thank you from the very bottom of my heart of hearts.

My street team: You ladies (and Nathan) seriously rock my world. The naked men threads in the middle of the night are an inspiration and your not-always-kind words are the kick in the ass that I need more often than not. Not to mention all the crazy wild pimping you do for me.

To the book bloggers: You guys are *seriously* the life-blood of the Indie community. None of us would be able to do this without you!

And to my fans; both new and old: Thank you. Thank you for taking a risk on a new author. Thank you for standing by the tried-and-true authors you love. Thank you for the late night messages in my inbox berating me for making you cry. Thank you for taking time out of your day to review my work and tell the rest of the world how much you loved (or didn't) it! From every author on the planet to every reader that ever has been, is, or will be: We love you.

For Amy
I'm singin' don't worry…

Prologue

I've been called a lot of things, starting with Porter Hale and going downhill from there.

I've spent my whole life trying to live up to the legendary reputation of my father—the man was a god amongst men when it came to his work. My mother did her best to make sure that our home life stayed out of the spotlight that constantly shone on him but sometimes there was just no helping it. Call it a hazard of the trade.

As the oldest of three brothers, it falls on my shoulders to set a good example and make sure my younger brothers, Parker and Preston, stay on the straight and narrow, right?

Well I suck at it.

Instead of sticking around to do the college thing like our mom had always wanted, I set off in Dad's footsteps. I wanted the fame and the glory and the parties with all the rock stars.

Not to mention the pussy.

So I ditched college after a few semesters, hopped on the old man's coattails, and started going by the name of Ryder. Ryder Ruff.

I know, I know: It's awful, but I can't change it now.

My brothers followed suit.

Turns out I filled my father's shoes and then some.

Industry headlines have dubbed us "The Princes of Porn."

We call ourselves the Dick Dynasty.

One
Porter

As my finger pressed down on the glowing yellow light of the doorbell, I adjusted the heavy leather utility belt around my waist and waited as the chimes inside the house finished their generic melody. Why they made me wear the stupid hardhat is beyond me, but it sat heavily on my head as the poorly sized plastic supports dug into my skull.

Honestly, a cable installer doesn't need a fucking hardhat.

The door swung open at last and a busty blond thirty-something woman in a nightgown ran a finger down the doorframe like it was made of the kind of wood that would harden at her touch.

It was all I could do not to roll my eyes at her.

"I hear you're in need of servicing."

"Please," she swept her arm to the side, "come inside."

I stepped over the threshold into the tiled entryway and choked back the scoff of disgust that threatened to escape from my throat. There are few things in this world that make me want to break shit: tacky décor is one of them.

The place was like something out of a nightmare: cream, gold, and honey-colored oak. The carpet was cream, the couches were cream with gold paisleys, and the god-awful wallpaper matched it. The entertainment center was the same colored oak as the baseboards and coffee tables.

The ceiling was textured like popcorn and had gold flecks of glitter in the white paint that hadn't been used since the seventies. A massive chandelier hung from the middle of the twenty-foot vaulted ceilings. The soft yellow lights burning in the sockets just made the entire space look dingy.

Porter

"My box is in the bedroom," she purred.

I followed the swish of her curvy hips down the hallway and bit down on my tongue. I was sickened by how over-the-top the silk and lace camisole was as it flowed behind her, rippling in the air with every step.

"I think it's back here," she leaned over a small computer desk that had been set up in the master suite, causing the silk to ride up her thighs and over the firm globes of her ass.

She wasn't wearing any panties and she was bent at the perfect angle to allow me access to her hungry slit.

"You didn't call me here to work on your cable box, ma'am." I pulled at the buckle of the tool belt and let it fall to the floor with a clatter that probably could've woken the dead.

She straightened and turned slowly, feigning ignorance as I slowly stepped toward her, "I'm sure I don't know what you mean!"

"I think you know exactly what I mean, Miss," I reached down and undid the first of the buttons on my low-slung denim jeans, "I don't doubt that you called me here to work your box—just not the one that plugs into the wall."

Her hand went to her throat as her eyes bugged out of her head and her mouth popped open. "Sir!" she shouted, "I am a married woman!"

"I don't see your husband around to service your box for you," another button undone, "you must be lonely here all by yourself."

Her hand dropped a little lower, pushing open the top of her nightie and revealing the swell of her obviously man-made breasts.

I closed the distance between us as I undid the last button on my jeans and used my hips to slam her into the desk she'd been leaning over. She gasped and pressed against my chest in a half-assed attempt to fight me off.

I could tell she wanted me though. They all did.

In a room full of women, all I had to do was snap my fingers and every single one of them would drop to their knees and pop their mouths open like miniature champagne bottles.

It was too easy. There was nothing real about it. I could feel myself going limp.

"Cut!"

David Michael

The director, Richard Dixon (I know), stepped out from behind his camera, "What the fuck, Ryder?"

I blew out a frustrated breath as the blonde draped herself on my shoulder, "I told you, Dick, you've gotta stop casting me with these dumb bitches that would love nothing more than to have me balls deep inside of them if you want the helpless damsel bit to feel real."

I peeled my mostly-naked co-star off me and made my way into the dining room we were using as a prep-room. Dick was hot on my heels.

"We don't pay them, or you for that matter, to act, Ryder. We pay you to fuck. That's it. So what's the problem?"

"What's the problem?" I pushed down the front of my still-unbuttoned jeans and grabbed my seven inches of limp dick, waving it at him like a Styrofoam pool noodle, "The problem is that even my pecker knows this is shit, Dick. You've got the biggest name in the porn industry on your project and you can't even bother to give me something half-decent to work with!"

"Actors!" Dick yelled, throwing his hands in the air, "Get me a fluffer in here! I need King Ruff ready in five minutes! No fucking excuses!"

I popped a few cashews into my mouth and watched him storm out of the room as a petite little brunette dropped to her knees and started working my piece with her mouth. She wasn't half bad. Assuming she could cope with the demands of the industry, she'd probably work her way from fluffer to female lead in good time.

My mind wandered as she went about her business and I went over my to-do list for the day. After the shoot, I needed to hit the gym and make sure I got some shopping in before hitting a premier party for Preston's latest flick.

With him being the youngest of us, I couldn't help but feel a little pang of pride at the name he'd made for himself. Parker had his own niche carved out in the more extreme circles of the industry, but Preston's, dare I say 'versatility', gave him a much wider market to work with—and the kid had worked it like a pro.

"Ryder! Get your hard-on in here and do your fucking job!" Dick's voice carried through the house.

4

Porter

The young thing bobbing on my knob pulled her head back with a pop and a smile as she wiped her mouth. Her big green eyes beamed up at me and I couldn't help but smile back at her, "Thanks, Kelly."

"My pleasure, but my name's not Kelly." She pushed herself to her feet and sauntered off toward the God-awful living room to wait for her next call to duty.

I tucked my hard-on back into my jeans and made my way to the bedroom where we were filming.

Get your shit together, Porter. It's go time.

I took my position between Blondie's thighs and waited for my cue.

"Action!" Dick's eyes were glued to his camera, ready for a show.

Blondie's hands came back to my chest and she resumed her half-assed attempt at pushing me away. I palmed one of her tits, hard enough that it'd probably bruise, and pinned her to the wall as I rolled on a rubber with my other hand.

"Your box is about to be serviced, as requested," I nearly choked on the cheesy line as I rammed my now-solid nine and a half inches into her as far as it would go.

"Ouch! Fuck!" she cried as I drilled into her again and again. It was the first believable thing that had come out of her mouth since the moment I walked into the house.

The drawers of the desk started to shake open as I slammed her into the wall again and again. Both hands were now kneading at her fake tits through the slip of silk she wore. At the rate I was going, the thing was probably going to end up on the floor in the next few thrusts, so I chose to be proactive about it and rip it off, leaving it wrapped around her arms and pinning her wrists behind her.

"Flip her around," Dick instructed.

I grabbed a fist full of her bleached hair as I pulled out and used it to spin her so that she was facing the wall. I straightened my arm, pressing her face into the gleaming surface of the desk, and slammed back into her from behind. The top of her head pounded into the wall in time to the thrust of my hips and I made sure to grunt every now and then so that it looked good for the cameras.

David Michael

I'm sure she was howling like a bitch in heat, but I was more concerned with the laundry list of shit I had to get done. I didn't hear any of it.

"Get her on her back on the floor."

Once again making use of the handle I had turned her hair into, I jerked her backwards, eliciting another sharp cry, and she all but fell to the floor to avoid further forceful handling.

I mechanically followed Dick's directions, straddled her right thigh, and threw her left calf over my shoulder.

I'm not sure how long we were in that position or how much rug burn ended up on her back, but Dick finally gave me the green light to finish and my mind came tumbling back to the business at hand.

"On her tits," he demanded.

I pulled the condom off with a snap and fisted my moneymaker; pumping myself toward the single moment they paid me for.

As my balls drew up close to my body, I pressed the fingertips of my left hand into the inside of my inner thigh and tried my best to block out the moaning, writhing mass of silicone and over-used flesh on the floor between my knees.

I felt my abs tighten and the familiar warmth spread throughout my body as the messy spray of come shot out of my dick and rained down on her tits, face, hair, and the floor around her.

She practically screamed in ecstasy, faking her orgasm to make Dick happy, and I shook off the remainder of my climax into her open mouth.

"That's a wrap, people!"

I pushed myself to my feet, grabbed my jeans off the floor, and walked to the bathroom to wash the rancid smell of her perfume and any of her stray juices off me.

"Money in the bank," I assured my reflection.

I wiped the lube from the condom off with the hand towel next to the sink, splashed some water on my face, and stepped back into my jeans.

"I'll be waiting for my check, Dick!" I yelled as I walked through the front door.

He might have shouted something back to me, but I took a deep breath of the warm southern California air and climbed in my Land Rover, blocking him out.

Porter

It was time to party with my brothers and that always turned out to be a shit show.

It's gonna be a long night.

I typed my destination into the built-in GPS and backed out of the driveway.

I needed to shop. There's nothing a new pair of Diesel's and a new beanie can't fix in my experience.

Except for maybe bad casting.

Two
Holly

"I'm a casting director for one of the largest agencies in Los Angeles County, Becks," I huffed out a frustrated sigh as I slammed my Audi A5 into park beside the curb, "a premier party for a fucking porno flick is the *last* place I want to be tonight!"

My best friend and long-time Devil's Advocate, Rebecca Sloan, growled into the phone, "Holly, I would give up my new set of tits—which I paid a pretty penny for, mind you—to have been invited to that party! And by Roman Ruff none-the-less!"

I felt my eyes roll around in their sockets, "Becks, his name is Preston. That nom de plume is heinous."

"I don't care what you call him, sweetheart. The boy is hot, he's loaded, he's hung, and most importantly, he's got two exceptionally good-looking brothers. I'd prefer Ryder, but I'll settle for Ryan if I have to. Your mission, should you choose to accept it or not, is to hook your best friend up. And since your buddy Preston happens to swing both ways, try and find yourself in bed with *two* really hot guys tonight so you can tell me about it all tomorrow."

The line went dead before I could protest any further.

I couldn't believe that I, Holly Nash, was about to walk into a premier party for a porn movie.

"What the hell is wrong with my life?" I asked my steering wheel as I pulled on the door handle. I swung my legs out of the car until my too-tall Jimmy Choos touched down on the asphalt.

I allowed the door to slam shut behind me and mashed the button on my key fob until the yellow lights flashed and my car chirped its acknowledgment, confirming the doors were locked.

Porter

I stared up the long drive lined with outrageously expensive cars and squared my shoulders. It wasn't like I'd never been to a premier party before. This was bound to be more of the same high-and-mighty my-dick's-bigger-than-yours hob knobbing that went on at any other industry function, only this time, the party-goers might actually be comparing their dicks.

Scenes from 'Eyes Wide Shut' flashed through my mind as I made the long trek up to the well-secluded mid-century mansion and it was all I could do to keep myself from turning around and bolting back to my car.

"You don't have to stay the whole time," I kept telling myself. "Just make an appearance, say hi to Preston, and get the hell out."

By the time I reached the six steps that led up to the columned front porch, I had miraculously managed to pull myself together. I tossed the long brown curls, which cascaded halfway down my back, over my shoulder, adjusted the silver necklace that hung low into the deep cut of my cleavage, and tucked my Michael Kors clutch under my arm. I was ready to make my entrance.

The door swung open before I could even reach the solid brass knocker.

"Holly!" Preston cried, throwing his arms out for a hug and kissing me on each cheek, "I'm *so* glad you were able to make it!"

"I wouldn't miss celebrating you for the world, Princess," I said with a smile.

Well shit.

With my say-hi-and-bolt plan ruined at the front door, I had to improvise. I needed to figure out how in the hell I was going to escape the night without getting roped into a gangbang with dudes in satin robes and scary masquerade masks.

Preston hooked his wrist through my arm and pulled me inside before I could come up with a reasonable excuse to drop dead on the veranda.

Tapeworm? Maybe I could just tell him I had a tapeworm and needed to go home because I forgot my medication. I wasn't entirely sure a tapeworm could be medicated though.

I could always take the hit to my ego and just claim explosive diarrhea. Nobody wants a guest with irritable bowels, right?

"I have a few people I want you to meet before I set you loose to explore on your own!" Preston's bubbling excitement pulled me away from my mental checklist of communicable diseases. I couldn't bail on him. He was too damn cute to crush.

"Lead the way," I acquiesced with a smile.

"Do you want a drink first? We've got a full bar. Granted, you might have to fight your way through my idiot brothers to get to it, but it'll help calm your nerves a little."

"What nerves?" My voice was about three octaves higher than normal and I felt a flush creep into my cheeks. "Is it really that obvious?"

"Let me guess," he put a finger to his chin and feigned contemplation, "You were fully expecting to walk in on some kind of massive orgy with projectors on every wall boldly broadcasting yours truly ramrodding some slut with fake tits while taking a dick down my throat, right?"

"What? No! I... You... It's not..." My tongue chose that moment to betray me as I continued to stumble over my words, unsure what I was supposed to say to that.

"Honey," he put a hand on my shoulder with a laugh, "you don't need to worry about that. My days of seedy release parties are *long* gone. I mean, I invite my *mother* to these things! I can't really have smut plastered all over my walls with her wandering around, can I?"

I could only raise an eyebrow at him as my eyes went to the full-frontal billboard-sized print hanging on the wall over his shoulder.

"Don't even!" Preston put a hand over my eyes, "*That* is art. You're comparing apples and oranges, my dear."

I bit my lip to stifle the giggle threatening to bubble out of my throat.

"You're insufferable, Holly Nash. Now *I* need a drink!"

He took my arm captive once again and dragged me through the thick crowd without so much as bumping into another person.

People called his name to get his attention as we passed, but he was a man on a mission and just waved them off with a smile.

"Oh good," he smiled over his shoulder, "my brothers seem to have taken a break from harassing my poor bartender. Marco!"

The gorgeous Latino hunk behind the bar turned from the glasses he was drying and beamed a mega-watt smile at the man whose grip still held my elbow.

"I was starting to think you'd never come back for me!" the bartender wailed.

Ugh. The good ones are always gay.

"Oh, honey, you know I could never leave you!" Preston leaned over the bar and planted a scorching kiss on him, tugging me halfway on top of the gleaming polished oak surface.

"Preston, with a piece of ass like *that* on your arm, I know you could leave me in a heartbeat. Who's the señorita bonita?"

I blushed before I could help myself as Preston gently trailed a finger along my jawline and down my neck to my collarbone, "This delicious little morsel is Holly Nash. I picked her up on a corner out in WeHo last weekend. Doesn't she clean up nice?"

"Preston, she's got about as much potential as a hooker as I do the Pope. Don't try to bullshit a bullshitter. Let's stick to things you know, honey. What can I get you and your pretty lady to drink?"

Knowing that something with an absurd amount of alcohol and sugar was about to be forced upon me, I choked back the urge to groan in protest and waited for Preston to spew a complicated list of ingredients at the bartender.

"Vodka martini. Dirty. Give us the goose."

Marco winked at Preston with a smirk and turned to mix our drinks, leaving me slightly awed that I wouldn't have to choke down some fruity concoction of juice and too many alcohols to count.

"Preston," I tried my best to look worried, "have you given up on drinking yourself to diabetes already? No Mai-Tai Ocean Breeze Sunrise?"

"The night is young, my dear!"

Marco placed two tall martini glasses brimming with olive brine and vodka on the counter and smiled, "Never-you-mind the secret ingredient."

Preston threw down a tip, snatched the glasses off the bar, and threw an arm over my shoulder, guiding me away before I could ask any questions.

"Do I even want to know what he meant by 'special ingredient'?" I eyed the glass next to my face warily.

"Like the man said, never-you-mind," he released me from his grasp and handed me my drink before lifting his own in a toast, "To my penis. May it continue to make me enough money to pay for these parties!"

I could feel the heat in my cheeks as I touched my glass to his and took my first sip of the cloudy, salty drink. Thankfully, I detected nothing but the sharp bite of vodka and the bitter, but satisfying, zest of olive brine.

"Hear, hear!"

I turned to see who had so vehemently joined in on our toast, teetering on my heels.

The sight of his five-foot ten-inch frame, clad in a light blue fitted t-shirt, dark blue, almost black, Diesel jeans, a pair of black and white high-top Converse sneakers, and a black beanie sporting the DC Shoes logo sent a flood of heat through my stomach.

Porter was *so* much hotter in person.

The dark stubble on his square jaw stood in sharp contrast to his intense ice-blue eyes and I was powerless to stop the images of his lips trailing their way down my body as his tongue flicked out to moisten his bottom lip before he spread them to reveal a gleaming row of perfect teeth.

The quiet moan that resonated in the back of my throat pulled me out of my reverie and my whole body turned red with embarrassment as I prayed that nobody else heard it.

"Porter!" Preston yelled from my side, "Where the hell have you been hiding?" His excitement over seeing his oldest brother seemed to be on par with that of my vagina. If he had started weeping with joy, I might've mistaken them for one another.

Porter

"I had to sneak out to the guest house and get a look at the reason we're all here!" They embraced in a very manly hug, back pounding and all, before Porter turned that glistening, predatory gaze back to me, "Who's your friend, little brother?"

"Holly Nash," I managed without collapsing to the floor like a swooning debutante. I extended my hand to him, mustering the best smile I could without looking like a mental patient.

He clasped it in his own, massive palm, and bent down to touch those sultry lips to my knuckles without breaking eye contact.

The electric pulse that shot through my body stiffened my nipples and dampened my panties.

"Pleasure to meet you, Holly Nash. I'm Porter Hale."

I thanked the Heavens above that my tongue had been stupefied by his surprising display of chivalry because I hadn't been able to say something stupid like, "I know who you are."

"Holly's *my* date tonight," Preston proclaimed, wrapping his arm through mine and pulling me against his side, "No touchy!"

"I'm sure you could spare one of your dates for your big brother," Porter pouted out his bottom lip and batted his lashes, "I promise to take good care of her."

"Go prowl somewhere else, you douche!" Preston laughed, "This one's a keeper. I'm not gonna let you chase her off."

He dragged me away from the eldest Hale brother and I noticed that the further we got from him, the more of my brain I seemed to have control of. I made a mental note to stay as far away as possible for the sake of my own well-being.

"Don't let his public persona fool you," Preston confided, "He's actually a great guy. He'd go into the depths of hell and back for those of us who make it into his good graces."

"Hmm," was the best reaction I could come up with.

The last thing I needed in my life was a one-night stand with a porn star.

I just had to convince the traitor between my thighs to agree with me.

Porter Hale was trouble.

Three
Porter

I reached down and pulled the hard-on inching down my leg into an upward position and pinned it in my waistband, a trick I had learned in middle school to disguise those inopportune boners that popped up as I nervously made my way to the front of the class.

"Who's the babe with Preston?"

I hadn't heard him sneak up, but the voice was a familiar one and I didn't have to take my eyes off Holly's ass as she walked away to know that it was Parker.

"Holly," I informed our middle brother, "and I'm gonna do bad things with her."

"Send her my way when you're done!" Something in his voice caused me to finally pull my attention away from the high hem of Holly's dress and the way it rose up just a tiny bit with every step she took in those sinfully high heels.

Parker and I are the same height and close to the same weight. His frame is a little bit broader than mine though, so he could probably afford to gain a few pounds. He always looked a little bit gaunt if you could see past the well-defined muscle, perfectly chiseled jawline, and shaggy, golden-blond hair.

He was the only one of us that took more after our mom than our father. He had her hair, her mouth, her perfectly straight, slightly upturned nose, and her long, thick lashes. His eye color, like Preston's and mine, was that of our father's: icy-blue.

The color made it easy to spot his dilated pupils.

"Really, Parker?" I questioned, trying to keep the accusation out of my voice.

Porter

"What?" His eyes snapped to mine and blazed defensively.

"You're high as a kite right now. I'm not stupid," I hissed the words in his ear so that other guests wouldn't overhear, "Couldn't you, for *one* fucking night, keep your shit together and support your baby brother?"

"I'm fine!" he said in an attempt to placate me, "It was just a little bump. No harm done. I'm cool."

He brushed absently at his nose as his eyes scanned the room around me. They darted from face to face, never staying long enough to actually *see* anything. He was just trying to avoid eye-contact with me.

"You're something else, Parker." I turned away from him and stormed off through the crowd, ignoring the cries of co-workers and fangirls alike as I made my way to the front door. I needed some air.

I know he's an adult, and in our industry, there are *far* worse drugs he could be addicted to, but he's still my little brother. I guess I just can't help but feel that I fucked up along the way somewhere and that some small part of me is responsible for him. Recreational or not, I hated that he had to be coked out of his gourd to deal with people. As the oldest, it's my job to step up and make sure that my brothers were safe. It's my job to make sure that they're taken care of. It's my job to keep them from making stupid decisions and ruining their lives.

I needed to be a better role model, be more involved. He needed my help to get that shit out of his life for good. I should've—

"You okay?" the concern in Preston's voice cut off my self-destructive train of thought before I could drive myself over the edge.

"Yeah," I huffed and waited for him to call me out on the poorly delivered lie.

"Bullshit," he set his beer at the base of one of the tall pillars of the porch, "What did I miss? When I left you by the bar, you were all but busting a nut in your jeans over Holly. Now you're out here rage-pacing by yourself in the driveway."

"It's nothing, Preston. I just needed some air." I couldn't bring myself to break the news to him that our idiot brother was high on coke that he'd probably sniffed out of some whore's bellybutton in a bathroom.

"You're pissed that Parker snuck off to get high, aren't you?"

My heart squeezed painfully inside my chest. I hated that Preston knew. I hated even more that he was so calm about it. The fact that one of his older brothers was high so often that it was normal to him made me feel even worse. How had I let this happen?

"When did you become so observant, Preston?" I threw an arm around his shoulders and we stood there at the bottom of the steps staring down his car-lined driveway.

"I always have been," he said with a smile, "How do you think I stayed out of trouble as a kid? You and Parker made it easy enough. All I had to do was watch the two of you and take notes. Every time you guys got caught doing something you weren't supposed to do, I figured out how I would do it better when it came to be my turn. Come to find out, I was usually right."

"Not always," I chided, "You followed us into this mess of a profession, after all."

He smiled at me with genuine happiness shining brightly in his eyes, "I did. And it has afforded me a life that most people only dream about. Look around you, Porter. I earned all of this. I'm the king of this domain. And all I had to do was sleep with a few skanky bitches and take some terrifyingly large dicks in the ass."

I drew my brows together and scowled at him, "That's *all*? That's a pretty high price to pay if you ask most people, Preston."

Preston laughed and ducked out from under my arm, "We're not most people, Porter," he said with a smile, "and not all of the bitches were skanky and not all of the dicks were terrifying. For the most part, I love my job. Especially now that I have a name for myself and I can be a bit more selective when it comes to who I work with."

I recalled my own workday and cringed, "I wish I could say the same thing."

"I keep telling you, man-on-man is where it's at! I make triple the money when I bottom, bro. You wanna make the big bucks, you gotta go where they pay."

16

Porter

It was a conversation we'd had several times over the years and it always ended the same way.

I screwed up my face and covered my ass with both hands, "Not a chance. Just the thought of getting pounded in my man box makes me want to cry."

"It's not that bad. Stop being a pussy. I know a few guys that'd be happy to break you in gently!"

"I'll pass, thanks," I shook my head, trying to Etch-a-Sketch the visual away.

"If you ever change your mind, let me know. I'll make some calls."

Before the conversation could get any further off course, heavy bass began thumping through the speakers in the house.

"Looks like Parker found the stereo again. We should probably get back in there before he trashes my house. Again."

I nodded in agreement, "He's an asshole and not good for much most of the time, but the man knows how to work a crowd. He'll have them in a frenzy in no time."

We stepped into the dining room where Preston always set up the bar during his parties. Parker had managed to set up a miniature stage, lost his shirt, and gathered a small group of women and gay boys to squeal at him while he danced. Dollar bills were quickly piling up at his feet and forming a hula skirt of sorts at his waist.

"Leave him be, Porter. He's harmless for now. Let him dance it off and have some fun." Preston had to shout over the tooth-chattering hit of the bass, but I got the message loud and clear: He didn't want to cause a scene.

If there's one thing our brother is good at, it's causing a scene.

"I need a drink." I turned on my heel and before I could take two steps, slammed into someone, nearly knocking her over. Her squeal as she teetered backwards had my arm shooting out to catch her before she could crash to the floor with her martini.

Holly lifted her head and shot me an accusing glare. There was so much anger blazing in her eyes that I half-expected her to shoot laser beams at my head.

It made my dick hard again.

"I'm so sorry, Holly," I apologized lamely.

"I know you're probably used to using people as doormats," she spat, "but you *do* know that's just a figure of speech, right? You should probably watch where you're walking." She shook the spilled booze from her arm and stormed off toward the front door as Marco appeared to clean up the broken glass.

"Fuck me!" I yelled as I sidestepped Marco.

I hit the bar with a vengeance and poured myself a triple shot of Jack, which I tossed back like a college boy.

I'm going to regret that in the morning...

I put away two more before leaning down on the polished bar top and glowering in the general direction of the stage, invisible through the throng of adoring fans trying to stuff dollar bills down my little brother's pants.

"What's wrong, Peanut?"

The nickname brought a sentimental smile to my face even as I rolled my eyes.

"Nothing, Ma. It's just been a long day."

"Don't you bullshit me, Porter Joshua Hale. I've been reading between your lines for thirty-two years, young man. Something is bothering you and you're going to tell me what it is."

I've always had a weird Pavlovian response to the use of my full name. When I was a kid, I knew I was in deep shit if she threw in the middle name or, God help me, the words "Just you wait until your father gets home!"

My whiskey-muddled brain fired in a furtive attempt to come up with a placating statement that would get me off the hook.

"I'm worried about Parker is all," knowing that she could sniff out a lie better than a drug dog could sniff out my brother, I had to go for a light version of the truth.

"You mean his drug problem?"

I couldn't mask my surprise and felt my eyebrows shoot so high they damn near joined my hairline.

"Don't look so shocked, Peanut. I was married to your father for twenty-eight years, God rest his soul. I know what this industry does to people. Honestly, I'm just thankful that only one of you struggles with it. Your father used to come home from parties just like this one higher than a kite. Parker's lucky to have you looking after him. If anyone can talk some sense into that boy, it's you. You always could."

"No pressure or anything," I muttered under my breath, praying that the deafening pounding of the speakers would keep it from reaching her ears. No such luck. The woman can hear conversations in China if she puts her ear to the ground.

"There shouldn't be pressure to be who you are, Porter, and you are his big brother whether you like it or not. Do what you do best and take care of them. I won't be around to do it forever, you know."

"Neither will I, Ma. When is it time for him to start acting like an adult?"

"About ten years ago, Porter. He hasn't had many role models in that department though. He's got some catching up to do."

Her voice was soft, but those words were sharper than any knife she could have buried in my chest. She gently patted me on the back and kissed my cheek before she wandered off toward the kitchen; presumably to gather her purse and jacket before heading home for the night.

"What the hell did you do to Holly?"

"Jesus Christ, Preston! Can I catch a break? Five minutes! That's all I ask! Five fucking minutes without being grilled by a family member about my failures of the evening!"

My youngest brother raised an eyebrow at me and caught his bottom lip between his teeth.

"Mom found you, didn't she?"

I blew out a long breath and rubbed my hands over my face, "Yeah."

"Queen of guilt trips strikes again!" he stepped around the bar and poured us both a shot from the bottle beside me, "Let's drink about it."

We touched our glasses and swallowed the whiskey in a single gulp.

"Really though," he poured two more shots, "what'd you do to Holly?"

I pressed my hands to my eyes, not wanting to think about the pretty brunette with an invisible leash around my dick, "I kinda broke her martini when I trampled her."

"That's it?" Preston paused with his shot glass half-raised.

"Yeah. I apologized, but she was pissed and stormed out."

"Weird."

"Yeah."

"You should call her tomorrow and apologize again." He set his empty shot glass down in front of him and slid a business card to me, "She's not usually so easily shaken."

My stomach sank when I read it.

"Are you shitting me?" I asked as the panic set in.

"Nope. Make amends." The little shit walked off without another word.

"Fuck me." I downed the shot he had left in front of me and stared down at the business card.

Holly Nash it read in bold black letters *Casting Director*

The name of the company was one anyone on either coast would recognize.

I had spilled a martini on a casting director with the largest casting agency in Hollywood.

Vodka-soaked olives had literally crushed my dreams.

Four
Holly

I flopped down onto the couch with a dramatic flourish and a groaned loudly.

"Stop it, Holly. It can't have been *that* bad." Becks set the glasses of wine she had chased me through the kitchen with on my glass-topped coffee table.

"It *was* that bad," I corrected her, "and get some fucking coasters."

She ignored my request and shoved my feet off the couch so she could sit down, "Only *you* could attend a party with the three hottest men on the planet and find a reason to storm out without saying goodbye."

I was beginning to regret my decision to call in the cavalry.

As my best friend, she should've been agreeing with whatever bullshit was coming out of my mouth, nodding sympathetically, and gasping at all the right times. The person sitting by my feet staring at me expectantly couldn't have been *my* best friend. Someone had taken *my* Rebecca and replaced her with a doppelganger. I had stepped into *Invasion Of The Body Snatchers* and my best friend had been replaced by an alien, hell-bent on taking over the human race by replacing us with mindless clones.

"Who are you?" I asked accusingly, "And don't make any sudden movements or I will kick you in the face with my deceptively fashionable designer heels."

"You're being a baby, Holly. Use your words and tell me what happened."

David Michael

I sat up and snatched my glass of wine off the coaster-less glass surface and threw myself against the back of the couch like a pouty five year old.

"He is evil and must be destroyed."

"Who?" the best friend thief leaned forward to retrieve her own glass.

"Porter Hale. He is Satan incarnate and we should call the Vatican right now and have them send an exorcist."

Becks' clone snorted into her wine glass, "You want the pope to exorcise a porn star? I mean, the dude's pretty liberal as far as popes go, but I don't think he'd go for that."

I took another gulp of my merlot before continuing my tirade, "For the sake of our own species, we'll have to take it upon ourselves then. He has some kind of supernatural demonic voodoo power that saps your brain cells and makes your vagina turn against you. One look from him and you go completely stupid. You find yourself dashing for the nearest Depends to keep yourself from leaking down both legs."

"Finally getting to the juicy stuff!" the Rebecca-bot taunted, "Go on." She folded her legs underneath her and watched me with those inhumanly joyous eyes over the rim of her wine glass—which was suspiciously full still, further confirming that she wasn't actually *my* Becks.

"You're a bitch and I hate you," I spat as I emptied my glass and rose for a refill. Rebecca-bot stayed on her perch while I considered running out the front door and leaving her to sit there waiting for me to return. Her batteries would run out eventually, right?

"What about Ryan and Roman?" she shouted after I had made my way into the kitchen.

I just rolled my eyes and pored my wine.

"They were fine," I huffed and returned to my seat, "*Preston* and *Parker* don't seem to be of the same tainted bloodline. Preston was his usual flirty self and Parker was too busy taking off his clothes and shaking his ass to even notice that I was there. Hard to notice a stranger when your pants are stuffed full of dollar bills."

Porter

"Uuuuuuugh!" Becks groaned, squeezing her thighs together and pinching her eyes shut, "Of course I would miss that! Next time you get invited to one of those parties, you *better* get a plus one! Otherwise I will have no choice but to follow you, scale the security fence, climb a rain gutter, break a window, and infiltrate with my mad ninja skills."

I laughed at the scene that played through my head as she spoke and felt some of the tension drain out of my shoulders. The paranoid delusion that my best friend had been swapped out for an alien robot fungus-clone quickly faded and I put my feet in her lap. I tipped my head back against the armrest on my end of the massive chocolate colored leather sofa and closed my eyes.

"Seriously, Becks, that guy fucked up my pussy. It took on a life of its own and all but jumped on his leg like an overly friendly Labrador."

She rubbed a hand over my freshly-shorn shin and clicked her tongue, "Aww... Tell Becks all about it." She took a sip of her wine and smacked her lips, "And don't bother sparing me the X-rated details."

I recounted my sex organ's hostile takeover of my brain in detail for her. When I got to the part where he smacked into me and spilled my drink, she finally gasped out loud and spoke for the first time since I'd started my story, "He *caught* you? You were crushed against his body? Did you cop a feel?"

"For fuck's sake, Becks! No! I certainly did *not* cop a feel! My pussy was on fire and my brain was telling me to lie down on the floor, pull my dress over my head, and beg him to ravish me! I did what any respectable woman would do! I yelled at him for being a clumsy oaf and stormed out with what little dignity I had left!"

Her mouth dropped open and she stared at me like I had started speaking Japanese. I left her just like that as I rose to refill our wine glasses. She still had the same look of shocked horror plastered to her face when I returned and set our glasses down on the ceramic coasters she refused to use.

"You have lost your fucking mind, Holly. You haven't had sex in, how long has it been now? A year? Two?"

"Three."

She whistled low through her teeth, "You haven't had sex in three years and the first man to have any kind of impact on your clit has you crying for exorcism? You're broken, honey. I don't know if I can fix this."

"Why do I call you in an emergency?" I groaned.

"I ask myself the same question every time. It's not like I've ever been good at the coddling thing you seem to crave. I'm going to tell you the same thing I do every time your libido rears its pretty little head and scares you to death: Plug the leak with a dick and quit bitching."

"That's your advice for everything," I countered.

"It's good advice. You should take it sometime."

"I want the Rebecca-bot back."

"Huh?"

"Nothing." I buried my face in my wine and reveled in my underhanded win.

"Really though," I said at length, "do you think the Vatican would send someone?"

"We're not Catholic."

"They don't know that."

"But God does and He's pretty tight with the pope from what I hear."

"You're probably right," I pouted into my wine glass for a moment.

It was then, as I stared into the swirling burgundy of the alcoholic grape juice in my hand, that I had an epiphany, "Catholics drink wine, right?"

"I don't like the sound of this," Becks replied warily, "but yes."

"Where do I join? Do I have to get baptized? And if so, do they just hit me with the metal thing full of holy water, or do they actually have to dunk me in a river? I think I could handle the metal thing, but there's no way in hell you're getting me in the L. A. River."

"Oh my God, Holly. You're paranoid. Stop it. We're not joining the Catholic church just so the pope *might* send an exorcist to banish the imaginary demons from your porn star."

"He's not *my* porn star!" I shrieked, mortified, "If anything, he's *your* porn star! You're the one obsessed with the whole damn family! Maybe I should have *you* exorcised for good measure!"

Becks held up her hands in a "don't get crazy" gesture and leaned away from me as far as the couch would let her. "I'm just trying to be the voice of reason here, Holly. You're a little off your rocker at the moment and it's time to come back down to earth. I'm not possessed. Neither is Ryder. And you can't join the Catholics. You don't have enough guilt to be Catholic."

She had a point on the guilt issue. I was notorious for being the "good girl" out of all of our friends. I have never been in trouble with the law, I'm not a whore, I never go out drinking on a work night, and my tits and ass are *generally* completely covered. I really haven't ever done anything to be guilty about—at least not by Los Angeles standards. The worst thing I ever do is lower my eyes and sprint like an Olympic runner when a homeless person asks me for money.

Add dirty people clothed in trash bags to my list of irrational fears—right below demonic porn stars with the power to melt panties with a glance.

"Have sex with him, Holly," her eyes bored into me with all the seriousness of a funeral director, "What's the worst that can happen?"

"AIDS!" I shouted before I could stop myself.

My best friend immediately spewed her mouthful of wine like a miniature, rose-tinted old faithful.

"Dammit, woman!" I screamed as I jumped off the couch, "Towels! We need towels! Paper ones! In the kitchen! Go get paper towels out of the kitchen! Hurry up before it sets in and stains anything!"

Looking back, I have no idea why I just stood there with my glass of wine in my hand, doing the Flash Dance, and flailing a limp wrist in the general direction of the volcanic wine spill, but it happened and I'm not ashamed. I blame the hormone overdose and too much wine.

Becks scrambled off to the kitchen giggling and returned with tears in her eyes, gasping for air, with an entire roll of paper towels. We quickly wiped down the leather and the hardwood, making sure we took care of anything porous before we went to work on the glass.

I can confidently accredit my friendship with Becks to one thing: her infectious laugh. It's what brought us together when we first met, and it's still one of my favorite sounds in the whole world. By the time we finished cleaning up the last drops of wine, even I had surrendered to its power and giggled alongside her.

We sat there surrounded by soggy paper towels stained blood-red with wine and laughed until we cried from the pain in our sides.

"This," I gasped, "*This* is why I call you in a crisis. Can you write it down so we don't forget next time? Your 'plug it with a penis' line is getting on my nerves."

"Oh, I can write it down for sure, but I'm still going to give you the plug it with a penis line. It's a solid plan, really."

I finally slid into a horizontal position and removed my stilettos before laying my head in her lap and pondering, "Why does it always have to be the assholes that do this to me? For once, just *one* time, can my vagina lust after someone who isn't a douche yacht?"

She giggled again, "Douche yacht?"

"Yeah, you know," I rolled my hand in the air in front of me in explanation, "A douche canoe, but bigger."

"How the hell do you come up with this stuff, Holly?" She beamed a smile down at me and grew an extra head. I was staring up at two Rebeccas when I finally formed my slurred response.

"Just wine."

I woke up the next morning still using her thigh as a pillow. Becks had slid down at some point in the night with one of my throw pillows and slept peacefully behind me.

I couldn't stop myself from groaning as I sat up and waited for the world around me to stop swimming. There was an obnoxious ringing in my ears and my eyeballs felt dehydrated.

"You need to be quiet now," Becks groaned, "it's too early for all that noise."

"I didn't even—" she held up a hand to silence me.

Porter

"Shh."

I blinked a few times and squinted against the sunlight reflecting off the polished wood floors. I had never been so glad to have a day off in my life.

I climbed to my feet, using the couch as a crutch. The gentle squeak of the leather beneath my weight infuriated my slumbering best friend.

She lumbered grumpily to her feet and stomped across the room, "You'll find me in your bed. Unless the building is on fire, leave me there."

I considered following her for a moment. Spending an entire day horizontal with my eyes closed sounded like a fabulous plan. I gave in to the call of a glass of water instead. My body was begging to be rehydrated and I knew that if I laid down in my bed it would be another eight hours before I put any kind of non-alcoholic fluid inside me.

I downed the first glass in a single breath. When my stomach didn't recoil to the point of expulsion, I filled a second and sipped at it as I headed for the driveway to retrieve my newspaper.

I said a quick prayer that my neighbors would still be asleep at bright-o'clock on a Sunday morning and dashed out for my weekly dose of the L. A. Times.

I dug my dead cell phone out of my purse and plugged it in before starting the coffee and settling in to read the paper.

I knew I didn't have more than a couple hours of peace and quiet before Becks woke up and regaled me with every minute detail of my drunken wailings from the night before. I had every intention of savoring each silent moment of blissful peace I could squeeze out of it.

I also hoped that the quiet practice of reading the paper would chase away the lingering images of bare skin and hungry mouths that had haunted my wine-induced sleep.

Porter Hale was an infection and I needed to find a cure. Fast.

Five
Porter

"What the fuck do I even say to her?" My head was pressed to my forearms and my eyes squeezed shut in an effort to keep out the glaring lights that seared like a laser beam into my brain, "Hey, Holly. It's Porter. Sorry I trampled you like an elephant?"

"You're really dramatic for a straight guy," Preston's voice was thick and groggy, but at least he was able to stand up and move around without dying, "Just call her and talk to her. It's not like she's going to climb through the phone and shank you with a sharpened toothbrush or something."

"She might," I griped, "I probably would if some dickhead plowed into me and spilled my drink then had the balls to call me the next day with some lame excuse."

"First off," Preston set his bottle of water down on the bar next to my head, "you shouldn't be drinking while you're getting plowed. I've tried it and it doesn't end well. I almost chipped a tooth. Second, don't give her a lame excuse. Tell her the truth. It's not like Parker really deserves to have you make excuses for him. He's an adult, Porter. He can deal with the consequences of getting coked out in front of dozens of people. Not your problem."

Our mother's words from the night before echoed through my brain and spurred a tiny worm of guilt for even considering outing his problem to a virtual stranger.

"I'll figure something out," I mumbled to the counter, "In the mean time, have you invested in a coffee pot yet? I've got a caffeine headache building on top of my hangover and I think my head might split open and spill my brains all over your bar if I don't get some java in me soon."

Porter

"Tough break, bro. You'll have to hit a Starbucks or something."

It took everything I had not to fall to the floor and cry at the thought of leaving the house without coffee.

"Before you crawl out of here like a half-drunk cockroach in search of your glorious caffeine, did you happen to see where Parker ended up last night? I checked both of the spare rooms upstairs on my way down and he wasn't in either of them. Did he take off with someone?"

I dug through the hazy memories from the night before and tried to remember where I had last seen him. He'd spent a good hour and a half stripping on his makeshift stage and then wandered off with half a dozen women hanging from him like jewelry.

"If I had to guess," I lifted my head and cracked an eye at the youngest member of our trio, "I'd say he posted up in the guest house."

"Ugh," Porter groaned, "He better not have fucked up any of my furniture. If the room is covered in a fine layer of dust, I'm gonna have to kill him."

I pushed myself to a standing position and waited for my precarious imbalance to pass before I spoke, "Want me to go out there with you?"

He eyed me warily, "You think you can make it?"

I thought about it for a moment before responding, "No, but I can crawl if I need to."

The genuine smile that split Preston's face was dazzling. All he had to do was smile and people fell in love with him. He just had one of those personalities that made you want to be around him. That smile was *his* moneymaker.

"Let's get to it then!" He wrapped an arm around my shoulders and, as much as I hate to admit it, I leaned into him to help steady myself against the almost-nautical sway of the room.

"I'm happy to help, Preston, but can we do this quietly? You hurt my head."

By the time we made it to the back door, I was feeling a bit better and my brain had begun to clear. I ducked out from under his arm as we passed into the expanse of his back yard and we walked along the edge of his pool side-by-side.

"Why do you think he does it?" Preston asked quietly.

"Does what?" I wasn't sure if he meant the coke or the extreme public cries for attention in which Parker was prone to participate.

"All the drugs and partying. I mean, we have it made, Porter. Look at this place," he waved an encompassing hand indicating his perfectly manicured property, "He could have all this too if he'd just stop being a dumb ass."

"Are you calling *me* a dumb ass?" I asked with a wink.

"No. I get why *you* don't go for this. It's not your style. I mean, your place is nice, but it's also very *you*. Sleek, modern, minimal. But Parker *wants* this lifestyle, he just can't afford it because he's constantly snorting his money and taking his glorified whores out to elite clubs. I guess I just don't get it. When does responsibility set in? When is he going to realize how much work and planning goes into having a place like this?"

"Honestly," I hooked my arm around his neck and pulled him into my side, "I don't know, kid. I've asked myself the same question for the last ten years. It's common sense stuff to most of us, but to him, he's just having a little bit of fun. He sees nothing wrong with it. After all, you and I get to have fun *and* have the nice things. Why can't he? He doesn't see the difference between once or twice a year and once or twice a week. I can't help but wonder where the hell I went wrong with him."

"*No!*" Preston stopped dead in his tracks, causing me to list dangerously to one side as I turned to face him, "You can't blame yourself for the bad decisions that asshole makes. I turned out just fine and you had to compete with *him* for the title of role model. If anything, I should have turned out more fucked up than he is by that reasoning. Let him take the blame for being a fuck-up. He's a big boy now."

"That's a lot easier said than done, Preston."

He sighed, clearly frustrated with me, then quirked his head to the side as if listening to a far-off voice. He groaned a few seconds later.

Porter

"If he's in there, I *really* hope he's alone and fully clothed."

The sudden change in topic threw me for a loop and I had to double-time it to catch up to him. His hand was already on the doorknob when I came up behind him and heard what he'd been listening to.

"Oh, gross..." I braced myself for the worst and hoped for the best. He turned the knob and the door swung open.

I was glad I had prepared myself for the worst.

"Are you fucking kidding me?" Preston screamed into the dim, sweaty air.

Arms and legs jolted to life and I counted at least six bodies, both male and female, scatter in every direction. Only one person remained in the center of the room as the rest of the party hurriedly poured themselves back into their clothes and slinked past us through the door.

The debut film that had given occasion to the party still played on the wall.

The prone figure of our middle brother groaned from his place on the floor. One of his hands reached out to the side, groping blindly as if it had a mind of its own.

"Your friends are all gone, fool," Preston spat as he made his way into the room, carefully picking his way over the debris and abandoned pieces of clothing.

"Well that explains why it's so cold in here," Parker mumbled as he rolled over onto his side.

"What the fuck is wrong with you?" Preston was dangerously close to Parker's head and his hands were on his hips, indicating he was going to flip out. I was about to bear witness to yet another brawl between my younger brothers. I knew I should step in and intercede, but Parker deserved what he had coming.

I crossed my arms and leaned against the doorframe, fighting off the grin that kept creeping onto my face.

"Outside of the raging hangover that you're not helping, I seem to be perfectly fine, if not a little bit nude."

"You just had an orgy to the soundtrack of your baby brother fucking his way through an entire cast! You are *not* perfectly fine! You're fucked up! I'm not sure which one of us needs

31

a shower more at this point! What the hell made you think it was okay to fuck your friends while watching me?"

Parker groaned as he returned to his position on his back and flung an arm over his eyes, "Can you try to leave quietly and close the blinds before you go shower? My head hurts."

That was the nudge Preston needed to send him over the edge. He swung his leg back and brought it down hard into Parker's ribs. The breath was still wheezing out of the drunk one when the shoe dropped again. I listened hard for the sound of cracking ribs with each blow. I'd step in at that point, of course. Until then, Parker was on his own.

I'd seen this play out more times than I could count. It never failed: Parker would overstep a line, Preston would finally snap and throw the first punch, then Parker would pounce like a tiger knowing that as long as he didn't swing first, neither of them would get in any real trouble for it. He would pound the ever-living snot out of our youngest brother until I finally stepped in and pried them apart.

Since Preston was the baby, he didn't get in trouble for starting it.

Since Parker didn't start it, he didn't get in trouble for defending himself.

Since nobody ever got seriously hurt, I was off the hook for not stopping them before it got physical.

Something about this fight was different though. Some sixth sense was buzzing in the back of my head and I didn't like it.

Preston's shoe was about to crash into Parker's chest for the fifth or sixth time when he froze. His foot hung there, suspended in the air a few inches from Parker, for several tense moments before he lowered it to the floor and narrowed his eyes.

"Get out," Preston hissed, "Get off my fucking property and don't bother coming back. I can't watch you do this to yourself anymore." He spun on his heel and stormed by me back into the yard.

As I stood there staring into the room, I finally realized why the familiar scene had bothered me so much: Parker hadn't even *tried* to fight back.

Porter

I pushed off the doorframe with my shoulder and strode toward him as he rolled back and forth on the floor clutching his ribs. Bruises were already forming on his naked skin. I could make them out even in the tenebrous light of the luxuriously large living room of the guesthouse.

When he finally caught his breath and stopped writhing at my feet, he let fly a string of curses that even I couldn't keep up with.

When he finished, I asked the question that had been burning in the back of my mind, "Why didn't you take him down?"

He stared at me with equal parts pain and anger shining through the tears that threatened to spill from his eyes.

"I know you could've," I pressed when he turned away to stare at the ceiling in silence, "I've seen you do it a hundred times before. Why not this time?"

I saw his body tremble as he choked back a sob. I had to fight the urge to walk away and ignore what had just happened. That's what I had always done before. I couldn't close my eyes to it anymore.

"Why, Parker?" I yelled, "What the fuck is going on in that head of yours? You just laid there and took the beating of a lifetime from a guy I've seen you wail on dozens of times. I want to know why, goddammit!"

"Because I deserved it," he whispered.

The tears finally slipped over the brim of his lids and traced wet streaks down his cheeks onto the carpet. Part of me felt bad for him, but a bigger part of me cheered at seeing him accept that he had messed up for once.

"I can't argue with that," I sighed, "Put some clothes on and let's get you out of here before he comes back with a sledge hammer to finish the job. I've got a phone call to make."

I rose to my feet and hit the power button on the projector near the door, erasing our brother's naked body from the wall before stepping out into the sunshine. I'd spent enough time dreading the call I was about to make.

My family was a train wreck. Preston had just tried to kill Parker, my mom had detached herself from our lives in almost every way, Dad was dead, and I was about to have a panic attack over calling a girl.

I felt like a foolish ass as I fished my phone and her business card out of my pocket and dialed the number. I forgot how to breathe as my finger hovered over the 'call' button and I tried to convince myself that making the call was worthwhile.

"If you don't push the damn button, you'll never know," I told myself and touched the little green phone symbol.

I put the phone to my ear and said a small prayer.

My stomach sank when the call went straight to voicemail.

Six
Holly

"You are a fucking mess, Holly Nash."

The encouraging words from my half-zombie best friend had me folding down the top half of the Sunday funnies to glare at her.

"Get some coffee, you grumpy bitch."

She shuffled her way through the living room and into the kitchen, yawning and stretching as she went. Her flaming red hair looked like a flock of pigeons had nested in it over night and she wasn't wearing anything but an emerald green bra and a silk g-string to match.

I turned my attention back to my comics while she went through the laborious process of ruining her coffee with precisely three tablespoons of sugar and a quarter cup of cream. She was *so* picky about her coffee that she had brought her own coffee mug to my house so that the coffee-to-junk ratio wasn't ruined.

How she managed to keep her figure was a mystery to even the wisest of cardio queens.

As expected, my grumbly best friend and her miniature bucket of coffee flavored sugar milk joined me in short order. It only took two sips before she jumped into her play-by-play of my drunken temper tantrum from the night before.

I kept my face schooled in a mask of cool indifference, but on the inside I grew more mortified with every word out of her mouth. I could only pray that I hadn't had a melt down of that caliber before I had left the party. I needed to call Preston and see if he could fill in any holes for me.

I was pretty sure I hadn't been blackout drunk until the bottle of wine, but I'd rather be safe than sorry.

Becks finally stopped talking to breathe and take a sip of her latte. I pounced on the opportunity to derail her.

"I know I've said it a thousand times before, but I mean it this time. I'm never drinking again."

She snorted into her nearly empty coffee bowl and rolled her eyes at me.

"You wouldn't do that to me," she announced as she rose to refill her caffeine supply, "Last night was comedy gold, honey. If anything, you need to be drinking more often."

I stood and followed her into the kitchen to retrieve my cell phone. If she was this happy about how much of an ass I'd been, I needed to text Preston and apologize profusely before I called him to figure out what I'd done.

I hit the power button and waited for the screen to flash to life. Every ounce of Becks' concentration was focused on making sure her scientific calculations were correctly executed, so I used the few moments of silence I had to practice the conversation I was about to have.

"Hey, Preston! Sorry I ruined your party last night... Let me know if I need to write a check or something." No.

"Hi, P! I hope I didn't break anything or throw up on someone last night!" No.

"Whatever happened, it wasn't me!" Tempting.

I suck at apologizing.

My phone buzzed to life in a frenzy of long and short vibrations as the push notifications from text messages, emails, missed calls, and voicemails began to come through. The drunken party girl side of me told me to just hit the power button again and walk away until I went back to work the next day.

The meaner, fun-sucking adult side won the day and I pulled up my email first.

It didn't take more than a couple flicks of my finger and a quick scan of the subject lines to ascertain that there was nothing that couldn't wait until Monday and closed the app.

Porter

Text messages were next on my list. Becks had wandered off to the living room again, so I read through them all and fired off responses to the ones that weren't business related. I promised myself the rest could be dealt with first thing the following morning.

I dialed my voicemail and put my phone on speaker as I turned to refill my own coffee cup. I dropped an ice cube into the steaming black liquid as I listened to the half dozen or so short updates about projects that had been green-lighted or cancelled in the twelve hours since I'd been on my self-appointed mini-vacation.

"I thought you weren't working this weekend." Becks was propped against the wall just inside the kitchen with her coffee cradled to her breast like an infant.

"I'm not," I pressed the nine button on my keypad to save the message for later and waited for the last of the voicemails to play, "I'm just checking my messages and making sure the world didn't end while I was ignoring my phone last night."

"Hey, Holly, it's Porter—er—Ryder. Hell, I don't know what you know me as," Becks and I exchanged surprised glances and she all but leapt on top of the counter to better hear what he was saying, "I figured I should probably call and apologize for last night. I was a bit drunk and pissed off at my idiot brother and I wasn't paying attention to what was going on around me and I didn't mean to run you over and I hope you can forgive me. If any damage was done when I spilled your drink all over you like a stumbling idiot, I'll pay to have it repaired, cleaned, or replaced. Whatever you think is best. I'd also like to take you out for drinks or dinner or something to say thanks for not stabbing me in they eye with the stem of your martini glass. We can go wherever you want, whenever you want, and I'll pay. Please let me know. Again, I'm so sorry for being such a total prick last night. I hope to hear from you soon."

He left his phone number and the message ended with a click.

Becks and I stood there gaping at each other in total shock.

Had he sounded nervous? He'd definitely been rambling.

37

David Michael

Before I had time to respond, Becks snatched my phone off the counter, ripping the charger out of the wall as she did so, and took off like a flash down the hallway. I heard the door to the bathroom slam shut and Porter's muffled voice begin to play once more.

She wouldn't...

Oh yes she would!

"Rebecca Sloan! You get your ass out here right fucking now!" I pounded my fist against the locked bathroom door and heard her giggle as Porter's voice repeated his telephone number. I put my ear to the door as I furiously and uselessly jiggled the door handle. She wasn't making a sound. I hammered my fist into the wood a few more times and yelled obscenities I didn't even know I had in my vocabulary.

My phone slid through the crack under the door and I heard her break into hysterical laughter.

I stared down at the tiny black square of glass, metal, and plastic at my feet.

What had she done?

I bent down and retrieved the device with a trembling hand.

The screen flashed to life when I pressed the unlock button and answered my question. My stomach sank as my mind raced to come up with a way to fix it.

I sank down against the wall opposite the bathroom door and sat there staring at the text message that was still on the screen.

Dinner sounds great. Friday. 7:30. Spago Beverly Hills.

I closed my eyes and pushed my head back against the wall. I knew at that very moment that I was going to have to fake my own death. Or possibly go out in search of some heinous crime to witness so that I could testify and go into the Witness Protection Program.

My phone chirped in my hand and I dropped it like it had transformed into a spider.

Porter

An eye appeared under the door across the hall, "What did he say?" I could hear the excitement in Becks' voice even with her face pressed to the floor.

"I don't know and I'm not going to find out," I said curtly, "I'm going to put you in my car, set it on fire, and drive it into the L.A. river. They'll assume the charred remains were mine and I can slip away to Mexico unnoticed."

"You're being dramatic, Holly."

"No, I'm being dead serious. I am *not* going on a date with a porn star. I have a career to think about. Can you imagine what the headlines of *'People'* would read? Ugh. That's not the kind of P.R. nightmare I want to deal with. No. Either you fix this, or your charred corpse is going for a swim."

"So," her eyeball disappeared from the crack beneath the door, "does that mean I can come out without you trying to hurt me?"

I kicked my phone back under the door, "No. You can fix it from there. The moment you set foot outside that bathroom, I'm going to bludgeon you with your own coffee mug."

"Well, I'll have to take my chances then because he says he can't wait to see you. I'll stay in here all night if I have to, but you're not getting out of this. You have a date with Ryder Ruff in just over twenty-four hours and, by God, I'm gonna make sure you show up for it."

I let myself slide sideways onto the cool hardwood and curled into the fetal position, "I hate you so much, Rebecca. You're going to hell for this."

"Thank me tomorrow," she responded from her self-imposed prison cell, "Oooh! Think I can get him to send a dick pic?"

I lunged at the locked door, sending her into a fit of cackling.

"It was a joke, Holly! Christ! Calm down!"

"It wasn't a joke and we both know it!"

"Well, it was *mostly* a joke," she admitted.

"I hope the toilet overflows on you," I spat with one final kick at the door, "It'd serve you right for being such an awful friend."

"It'd be *so* worth it."

David Michael

I left my post outside the bathroom and retrieved my coffee from its spot on the kitchen counter.

She had to come out eventually, and when she did, I'd be waiting.

Seven
Porter

Holly's text finally came through as I pulled into the gym and my first reaction was to call her and thank her for understanding. I didn't want to push my luck though, so I just shot back a short response and called Preston. He was always my go-to guy for all things involving women.

"Well, I guess I didn't fuck it up too bad," I said when he answered, "She agreed to meet for dinner this weekend."

"Really?" There was more surprise in the single word than there should have been and I knew something wasn't quite right.

"What do you mean, really? Why are you so surprised by that?"

"It's just, I dunno, I figured she'd forgive you, not set up a dinner date."

"Preston, it's *me*. I could go through the phone book and call every number in alphabetical order and a good ninety percent of the people I talked to, male *or* female, would agree to a dinner date with me."

"Trust me, I know, Porter. I was just sure she was in the other ten percent is all. She *hates* the porn industry. She was ready to bolt the moment I opened the door for her at the party last night. It's not her scene and she's kinda grossed out by it all."

Not her scene? *Everyone* likes porn. What the hell did he mean 'not her scene'?

"Porter, I gotta go," a loud slap interrupted Preston's goodbye, "You son of a bitch! You're not even inside me! There was no need for that!"

"Are you on set?" I asked, choking on the laugh that threatened to rumble out of my throat.

"Yeah, but this dumb son of a bitch can't manage to keep it up, so we're all just kinda sitting around while he grinds his hips into my ass. It's not like I have anything better to do with my day! Anyway, I think I'm gonna have to teach this straight boy to bottom so we can get the hell out of here before I'm too old to enjoy my good looks. I'll talk to you when we wrap."

"Go easy on the poor guy."

"One more slap on my ass cheek and I'll split the bastard in two."

The sharp crack of hand on flesh came over the line just before it went dead. I couldn't help but feel sorry for the guy. If he really was straight, he had just crossed a line he probably hadn't intended on crossing when he showed up for work that morning. Preston's dick is *almost* as big as mine and he had a reputation for getting a little bit rough with his bottoms. The potential for stitches was high.

I cringed as I tossed my phone into my gym bag.

The familiar sounds of clanking weights, grunting meatheads, and the over-caffeinated Jazzercise instructor welcomed me to the second best place on Earth.

I'll be the first to admit I'm a gym bunny. My body pays my bills and keeping it tuned up is part of my routine seven days a week.

I hit the locker room and changed into my loose pair of basketball shorts and a demolished t-shirt with the sleeves ripped off. I'm all about cardio, so I had to be able to move.

"Porter!"

I cringed before turning around to face Vanessa, the over-caffeinated Jazzercise instructor.

"Hey, V. How was class today?"

"It was great! Really invigorating! We miss seeing you in there!"

I'd had a momentary lapse in judgment a few months prior and found myself in her class a few times. All the bouncing tits and ass had been like a siren call to my over-imaginative loins.

Porter

I ended up hooking up with her once and never set foot in her class again.

"Yeah, it just turned out to be more of a hindrance for my training. It's good to see you though!"

I turned to walk away and she grabbed my forearm in a vice-like grip, "How about a spot?"

She walked to a nearby flat bench and loaded up the bar with a hundred pounds of iron.

Not wanting to offend her, I took my position over her head and gripped the steel bar on either side of her hands.

"Now this takes me back," she winked up at me.

The tip of my dick was dangling inches from her face and it took every ounce of my willpower not to roll my eyes and walk away as she stared at it absently licking her lips.

I hefted the weights out of the bar catchers, drawing her focus back to the task at hand, and let the bar settle into her palms.

Her form and breathing were flawless and her endurance admirable. I spotted her through four sets of twenty before she called it quits and allowed my to guide the bar back into its cradle.

"Thanks, Porter. If you ever need to add a little extra cardio to your day, you know where to find my bed."

She leaned up on her toes and kissed my cheek before drifting off to the women's locker room.

I absently wiped the spot with my shoulder and headed for the nearest treadmill. The need to run was reaching a critical point.

I programmed in a two mile run at six miles an hour and hit start.

My body took over and quickly settled into the familiar rhythm. My pulse, breathing, and footfalls synched up perfectly and all thoughts of Vanessa were quickly pushed from my head.

As I pushed myself through the quick two miles, the stresses of the day sloughed off like dirty clothes. The booze from the night before poured through my pores in steady streams of sweat and left me feeling invigorated and pure.

When my warm-up run was over, I moved on to lunges, then weighted lunges, twenty-yard sled pulls, and leg presses. With twenty minutes to go, I headed back to the treadmill and hit the hill.

Six miles an hour with a five percent incline would push me just enough that I'd be exhausted, but still be able to walk the next day.

That last twenty minutes, I found myself with only one thing on my mind: Holly Nash.

I could still see her slender, incredibly long legs perched on top of those sky-high fuck me heels. The way her dress clung to her hips and showed off her tiny waist and powerful thighs was emblazoned in the forefront of my memory. I had spent most of the night thinking about them wrapped around my hips. Her perfect breasts with their deep cleavage and long slender arms tipped with delicate unpolished fingers had ravaged my dreams. Her plump, rosy lips and soft, supple tongue had worked my shaft with expert precision as she stared up at me with her incredible hazel eyes. My hands had been fisted in her impossibly soft auburn hair and I was moments from watching her swallow my load when Preston had shaken me awake.

Running became increasingly difficult as more of my blood found its way from the brain in my head to the one between my legs.

Cold shower. I need a cold shower.

The treadmill leveled out and I slowed to a clipped walk for the cool down portion of my final run. It was all I could do to put one foot in front of the other as I prayed my dick didn't get any harder.

When the belt beneath my feet finally came to a stop, I all but sprinted across the gym to the locker room and slipped into the first available shower stall.

The spray of cold water slammed into me like a truck and stole my breath away as it soaked into my gym clothes and filled my shoes.

"Get your shit together, Porter," I chastised myself as I kicked off my sopping shoes and tossed my soggy clothes into the corner.

Completely ignorant of the frigid stream dousing the rest of my body, my dick stayed stiff as steel and pointed accusingly at the shower handle.

Porter

Flashes of Holly's creamy skin sliding over every inch of my body played through my mind and I realized there was only one way to resolve the problem of my arousal.

I gripped my disobedient shaft and quickly worked my strokes into a brutal pace. The muscles in my exhausted thighs tightened more with every thrust of my bucking hips.

I felt the deep tightening in the pit of my stomach as my balls drew up against my body. I lost all control when my thighs finally cramped and my abs seized up to force my orgasm out of me like a gunshot.

"Fuck!" I yelled as my legs gave out and I dropped to my knees.

The tiles at eye level were covered in jets of my semen. My vision went fuzzy as my softening cock unloaded the rest of its payload into the drain at my knees.

My head spun around at the sound of the shower curtain behind me being ripped open. One of the personal trainers I had worked with on more than one occasion stood there in his gym shorts and company polo. He looked from me to the wall and then back to me before his eyes dropped to my ass and a grin flashed across his face.

"I thought someone was dying," he explained before turning away and closing the shower curtain behind him, "Clean up your mess before you leave, *Ryder.*"

"What the fuck is wrong with you?" I asked the smug piece of flesh, now napping between my burning thighs.

I reached up and increased the temperature of the water before halfheartedly tossing water at the wall in a sad attempt to rid the shower of any evidence left behind.

How the hell was I supposed to sit through an entire meal with her across the table from me? I couldn't even make it through an hour at the gym with her halfway across the county.

"This isn't going to end well," I muttered as the last of my ejaculation swirled down the drain.

Eight
Holly

"So *this* is what a Monday is supposed to feel like."

I had managed to make it to my office without turning around and climbing back under my blankets, but hadn't actually done any work yet. I sat there staring at my computer screen waiting for it to give me instructions on how to do my job.

"Serves you right for actually enjoying your weekend."

My eyes went to the doorway where my favorite member of my support staff was leaning casually.

"Shut it, Mitch. I liked it better when I didn't bother with silly things like days off."

Mitchel Michaelson, gay secretary extraordinaire, pushed himself away from the doorframe and strode into my office like he owned the place. He was one of the three people on the planet who could do so without losing life or limb. The other two were Becks and the man who wrote my paychecks.

"As your executive assistant, I have to agree with you. More shit gets done that way. As a gay man who loves to party on the weekends, I feel like I need to organize a festival to celebrate the fact that Holly Nash does indeed have a life outside of work."

"You're a bitch," I turned away from him and pretended to work on my computer.

"A bitch who's right. Now give me all the dirty details! How was the party? Did you get gang-banged while dozens of creepers stood around the room jerking off and filming it with their phones?"

I deadpanned him. He knew how ridiculous his question was and I wasn't going to warrant it with a response. Instead of

46

balking as I had hoped, he waved a perfectly manicured hand at me and continued.

"Did you at least get to see one of the Princes of Porn get his freak on? I mean, those parties are pretty legendary. I have this friend whose cousin knew this guy that went to one of them and totally got banged by Roman in the middle of the kitchen. Not a single appetizer was spared from their bout of pornographic passion. Rumor has it there's a tape of it out there somewhere."

"You're disgusting," it took everything I had not to smile at him, "I imagine there's a reason you came in here beyond just grilling me about the Hale brothers and their sexual practices."

"Nope," he rose from the chair he had draped himself across and made his way back into the hallway, "You should really work on your storytelling, Holly. It'd make my life much more interesting."

The soles of his steel gray Cole Haans snapped sharply on the marble hallway as he sashayed his way back to his desk. Moments later, the phone on my desk lit up and his voice boomed from the speaker, "Your two o'clock is cancelled, your two-thirty has rescheduled to three, and the producer for the new Michael Bay flick wants you to call him as soon as possible."

"Thank you, darling. I'd be lost without you."

"Don't you forget it!" The line went dead.

I absently scrolled through my emails and compulsively rearranged everything on my desk in an effort to convince myself that I was too busy to call the producer. Talking to the people behind the cameras is my least favorite part of the job. I get the scripts, I attend the meetings, I find the faces. That's my job and I'm damn good at it. I don't need some overbearing, half-psychotic perfectionist flaunting his budget in my face and telling me how to do the one thing I'm *really* good at.

When I had organized the crumpled up headshots in the garbage can under my desk, I finally admitted to myself that I couldn't justify putting the call off any longer. If I was going to get to my lunch break at a decent hour, I'd have to get it over with sooner rather than later.

I should've called sooner.

David Michael

After three hours of being lectured on the importance of the eye and hair color for the leading man and how it was imperative for the leading lady to have an impossibly tiny waist, it was a quarter after two. I had thirty minutes to find food, devour said food, and get my ass back to the office to prepare for the meeting I had at three.

I was nudging my way toward hangry and knew better than to go into a meeting with a potential client in that state of mind.

I had just bent to grab my purse and sprint for the parking garage when Mitch came strolling back into my office with a Styrofoam container in his hands.

He set it on my desk and walked away without a word.

I opened the container to find a BLT on whole wheat bread with a grilled chicken salad on the side.

I mashed the intercom button on my phone, "Remind me to give you a raise."

If he responded, I couldn't hear him over the sound of the perfectly cooked bacon being crunched between my teeth.

After devouring the entire sandwich and half the salad, I started to feel human again. I stopped shoveling food into my mouth like I hadn't eaten in days and took a more civilized approach to the last half of my lettuce and chicken. I picked up my fork and used *that* as a shovel instead of my fingers.

I sat back, sated and borderline comatose, as the urge to drink the last of the dressing out of the container dissipated.

"Your three o'clock just called to confirm his appointment." Mitch announced from the doorway, "He's about ten minutes out. Get your life together, wipe the ranch off your face, and for the love of Gaga, buy some granola bars to keep in your purse. You're a scary woman on a good day, but you turn into some kind of angry black hole for food when you're hungry and God help anyone who gets too close."

"I'll see what I can do. Can you grab me the script for this project? I want to glance through it one more time before I listen to this guy drone on for the next two hours about his 'artistic vision' and how his movie just *has* to star Angelina."

Porter

"And that bullshit is *exactly* why I just guard the door," Mitch spun on his heel, snapped his fingers out to the side, and shook his head. His inner diva always did a hell of a job expressing his distaste.

My phone vibrated on my desk as Mitch dropped the miniature manuscript on my desk.

"Thanks, Snookums."

"Mmmmhmmm," was the only response I got as he flitted back to his desk.

I decided the text message would be more fun than a read through of a script that was doomed to be completely rewritten at least three times during production.

I'm bringing The Kit to your office on Friday. No time to change at home before your date with Ryder.

I groaned and shoved the phone off the edge of my desk. The three hour phone call and light-speed ingestion of my lunch had driven all thoughts of my impending 'date' with Porter Hale to the darkest corners of my mind. I might have actually gotten lucky enough to forget about it entirely. Then I could have just texted him the day after with a lame excuse about work being too busy and we would have been even. He spills my drink, I let him sit alone in a restaurant for an hour, and we never have to speak again. It seemed like a pretty good pipedream at the time.

Then Becks happened.

Her and that damn kit.

She always ruins my fun.

The Kit had made its first appearance at our senior prom. I hadn't intended on going at all. I'd bought a few pints of ice cream and a stack of the latest chick flicks. Then a crazy ginger girl dressed to the nines showed up on my doorstep with a dress and corsage in one hand, and an ominous duffle bag in the other.

"Please tell me we're not burying your date's body already," I had said with a suspicious glance at the massive black bag.

"No. He's still alive and well. He took off with your date to do God-only-knows-what while I try to salvage what's left of your dignity." The duffle hit the floor with a thump and several rattles. I remember feeling like prey caught in the crushing embrace of a human-sized snake as she pushed me down onto the couch and went to work.

A flat iron, round brushes, a blow dryer, dozens of shades of nail polish, eye shadow, lipstick, foundation (both liquid and powder), blush, files, buffers, tweezers, and something in a box that said *Summer's Eve* tumbled onto my parents' living room floor. Thankfully, the last one went back into the bag almost immediately.

It had taken just over an hour and a half for her to squeeze, tweeze, brush, blow, paint, and primp me into what she still calls 'The Prom Night Miracle'.

It was only the first of many run-ins with The Kit and I wasn't looking forward to another.

I glanced at the clock in the bottom corner of my computer monitor and squared my shoulders. I had five minutes to make myself look presentable and get to the conference room where the meeting was to be held.

Lucky for me, it was right across the hall from the executive restroom I shared with one other casting director.

I slid the deadbolt into place behind me and turned to study myself in the mirror over the sink. I blanched as I realized it looked as if I *had* decided to drink the ranch out of the container. I'd start there and work my way up.

I quickly wetted a paper towel and wiped the creamy mess away from my lips before digging into my purse for the spare tube of lipstick that years of being around Becks had taught me to carry. I recolored my lips and ran a brush through my slightly disheveled hair.

I had learned a long time ago that, in my line of business at least, less is more. I have good skin, dark, thick lashes, and natural volume to my hair that made blow dryers an unnecessary appliance in my house. If I put the extra effort into being girly, it never failed that the Good Ol' Boys mentality would take over and even the most liberal thinking man would treat me like a coffee fetcher.

Porter

Sharp, professional, and ballsy was the way I preferred to come across and it had worked well for me—much to Becks' dismay.

With my proverbial game face in place and a quick glance at my Tiffany's watch, I strode from the restroom without another glance at the mirror.

"Gentlemen!" I said with a smile as I entered the brightly lit conference room, "Let's get this party started, shall we? Can I have my assistant get you anything? Coffee? Tea? Water?"

Both men politely declined my offer and gestured for me to sit.

"We'll try to make this as painless as possible," the larger of the two men, Tyler Gainsworth, a man I'd worked with a handful of times before, said, "I know how much you love being told how to do your job."

"I appreciate that, Ty."

"I have to assume that you've read the script at this point," Nathan, the squirrely little red head Ty had introduced via email, interjected.

"Of course," I replied coolly, "I assume we'll focus mostly on Ashley and John then touch on the seven supporting characters, three female, four male, and then you'll propose a final headcount for extras, am I correct?"

Nathan was clearly new to the business and hadn't quite figured out that these meetings almost always followed the same format. He recovered from his surprise quickly enough and nodded curtly with a tight smile.

"Great," I said, just as tightly, "Let's get on with it. For Ashley, I see someone who appears to be in their early twenties with mid-length blonde hair; wavy, not curly. She needs to have big, green, innocent eyes and pouty lips. Very 'girl next door'. I see Taylor Swift without the twang."

Ty's eyes had lit up as I described his girl. I'd seen it a hundred times before. Whenever a producer finds someone else who can see his vision as clearly as he does, there's a fire that kindles inside them. It's a very dangerous fire that can burn out of control in a flash and completely derail a meeting for *hours*.

The idea of letting him detain me in an attempt to get out of dinner that night was a tempting one.

Sadly, I'd rather hang myself than be trapped in a room with a producer for any longer than absolutely necessary, so I pressed forward.

"John is a little more the bad boy type with a gentleman's charm. He's got the good looks and he knows it, but doesn't really rely on them to get him where he's going. We need tall. Six foot. Maybe six two. Short black hair and brown eyes. Tan and muscular, but lean as opposed to bulky. Oh, and he needs good hands."

I pulled myself up short at that point before I rambled on to the point of losing them. Tyler was already starry eyed and in love with both assessments and, by the surprised look Nathan hadn't been able to conceal, he was too.

With the big ones out of the way, I gave a quick run down of the minor characters and got an estimate for the extras head count before rising from my chair and ushering the two of them out the door before they could remember that they think they know what's best.

That was how my entire week went. Meeting after meeting with too many cocky, pompous, sexist dimwits who marched into my office to tell me how to do my job and got shut down at every turn.

Friday had finally arrived and as I all but shoved the last team of morons out of my conference room, the entrance at the opposite end of the room burst open to allow Mitch, Becks, and The Kit into the conference room.

"Sit," she commanded.

I briefly considered bolting out the door I had just ushered Ty through and begging him to hit the emergency button on the elevator between floors. I quickly abandoned the idea when I remembered that Becks is a ninja and would have caught me before I even made it halfway down the hall.

I begrudgingly shuffled my way across the room and unceremoniously dumped myself in the leather chair between them.

Porter

Before I could even groan about it, there were twenty fingers in my hair and I swear to God, Becks was unpacking The Kit with her toes.

"We have just shy of thirty minutes to get her out the door and on her way to The Hills. I've done more with less, but we'll be cutting it close none-the-less."

"Oh honey," Mitch crooned, "I can get a drag queen in full makeup and dress in less than fifteen. I bet we can have her done in twenty-five."

"I hate you both," I grumbled.

There was a queasy feeling in my stomach and the only way I could make it stop was to imagine Porter going through a similar form of torture.

Nine
Porter

"Christ Almighty, Lorraine!" I screamed at my stylist, "Don't you usually count down before you do that? Fuck!"

She just shrugged her shoulders before dropping the white strip of paper covered with wax and what used to be the hair on my balls.

"You want emergency appointment, I give you emergency service. No time for counting."

I had been going to Lorraine for all of my grooming needs since I was eighteen, but still had a hard time deciphering her thick Korean accent most days. It might've been the blinding pain that kept me from deciphering the words that came out of her mouth.

My ears were still ringing from her last tug when she dropped the ice pack on my groin with simple instructions even her accent couldn't muddle, "You keep there."

"Yes ma'am." Was my voice an octave or two higher than normal, or was it just me?

I pressed the freezing cold bag to my traumatized scrotum and laid on the table breathing as if I were in labor. There *had* to be a way I could get them to give me laughing gas before my next appointment.

"It's a good thing my junk is insured, Lorraine. I'm convinced you're going to tear the thing off one of these days."

"No," she said with a knowing grin, "I like your movies too much! Beaber Feber is my favorite!" She waggled her eyebrows at me and threw her head back with a laugh that made my skin crawl.

"Do you mean *Beaver Fever*?" The mispronunciation was a train wreck I didn't even want to think about.

Porter

"That's what I say! Beaber Feber! Don't you speak English?"

She went on a tirade in Korean that I could only imagine had something to do with stupid Americans and their inability to understand their own language.

I bit my tongue and let her do her thing while my balls finally came out from their hiding place just beneath my tonsils.

"You have hot date tonight?"

"Sort of," I sat up from the table and reached for the jeans around my ankles, "I mean, *she's* hot, I just don't know where it's gonna lead. Clearly, I *hope* to take her to bed, but she's not like other women. She's a bit hot headed and a lot guarded. It wasn't such a good combination for our first encounter. She's almost kind of scary."

"Ooh," she said with a solemn nod, "You really like her. I see."

"No!" I defended, "It's not like that at all!"

"No no no," the three words came out as one, "I see your eyes change when you talk about her. Is okay. You need to be careful though. Don't let her break my favorite client!"

She scampered through the door before I had a chance to convince her that I was only trying to get in with her casting firm.

I had already banged my way into one industry; I wasn't above doing it again.

I jerked my jeans up around my hips and fastened my belt before walking out into the lobby to pay the bill for my torture session.

"Always a pleasure, Lorraine," I said as I signed the credit card receipt.

"The pleasure is always for me," she replied with a wink.

My smile faltered and I waved awkwardly as she once again began to laugh at her own joke. She had an insane talent for making a run-of-the-mill appointment to wax my balls an intense exercise in awkwardness.

Unfortunately, she was the best, and I only used the best. Especially when my dick was on the line.

55

I slid my aviators back into place as I stepped onto the sidewalk and into the late-afternoon sun. I'd made it out of the appointment with time to spare and headed for my Land Rover.

As I drove, I tried to piece together how the impending conversation would go.

She'd still be frosty for sure, but even her ice queen act couldn't hold up against my charm for too long. I would just have to pour on the boy-next-door appeal and come off as harmless. If she knew my angle, she'd shut down in a heartbeat.

Holly Nash would definitely not fall for the bad boy porn star act that got me between most thighs. No, Miss Nash was going to take some work. Work that I fully intended on turning into a game.

With any luck, we'd both enjoy it in the end.

I pulled into the parking lot of the restaurant ten minutes before seven and parked in a stall at the back of the building. The mirror in the driver's side visor helped me soften my appearance a bit. I pressed my hair forward and the bangs up and to the side so that I almost had a pompadour. There wasn't much I could do about the scruff on my jaw, but the aviators had to go.

Those few simple changes made me less predatory and a little more innocent looking than I'd ever been in my life.

A clean shave would've been the perfect touch, but there was only so much I could do in the front seat of my SUV with only five minutes before we were supposed to meet.

After a final once-over, I locked up and headed for the front door.

"Can I help you?"

"I have a reservation for seven-thirty under Hale."

The gentleman glanced down at the podium he stood behind before nodding his head curtly, "Of course, Mr. Hale. Right this way."

I followed him to an intimate booth in the back corner of the main dining room.

"Shall I bring your guest straight back?"

"That'd be great. Her name is Holly Nash. She'll probably ask for me by name."

"Of course, sir. Your waiter will be right with you."

"Thanks, Jeeves."

I could see the change in his eyes the moment I said it and had to exercise every ounce of my self-control to not laugh in his face at my own joke.

The poor guy probably heard it all day long every day.

I made a mental note to tip well in hopes that he'd get a cut of it at the end of the night.

"Good evening, sir," a twenty-something gentleman in a crisp white button up and cheap black slacks gave me an award-winning customer service smile, "Can I start you off with something to drink while you wait for your dinner guest?"

"Water would be great for both of us and I'd also like a bottle of the best Merlot you have."

"Of course, sir. I'll have your water out right away and deliver the bottle when your guest arrives."

"Thanks."

He had recognized me. I could tell by the way he kept glancing down at my crotch. The only reason I chose fine dining over fast food was the fact that the staff were all so used to waiting on celebrities that they didn't get all fangirl crazy on you in public.

Usually.

I spotted Jeeves heading toward my booth with Holly in tow and my palms began to sweat.

What the fuck?

I never get nervous around women.

I wiped my hands on my jeans as I rose to greet her. Instead of the more intimate kiss kiss on the cheek that women tended to try with me, she went in for the kill with a very formal, very *firm* handshake. Her grip provided a sharp contrast to the sensation of her painfully soft skin beneath my fingertips.

The sensation shot a jolt of pure desire up my arm and straight to my groin.

"Thank you for agreeing to meet with me."

Such a lame fuck.

"It's no trouble."

Harsh.

She released my hand and sat down across from the table as the waiter returned with two glasses of ice water.

"Thank you," she nodded politely to the waiter, causing her hair to swing forward from where it had been neatly tucked behind her ear. Something inside of me wanted to reach out and smooth it back into place.

I was thankful I had refrained when she returned her gaze to me. I could practically see her walls slide into place as the ice replaced the warmth that had been bestowed upon our server.

"Why am I here, Porter?"

Her question caught me off guard and I could do nothing but stare at her in response.

"We both know you didn't agree to one of the most expensive restaurants south of San Francisco just to apologize for breaking my martini glass. I might not be as worldly as you are in some aspects, but I am far from stupid."

I had the good sense to at least pretend I was offended.

"Holly, believe it or not, there are good people in the world who do things for others just for the sake of doing the right thing. Not all of us have to find a motive to justify spending time with another person."

A glimmer of fire lit behind the glaciers in her pupils.

"I don't doubt that for an instant, Porter. What I *do* doubt is the fact that you are one of those people."

I didn't have to act offended after that jab.

"You don't know me at all, Holly. Who the hell are you to decide what kind of person I am?"

I could feel the steel of my own walls slide into place as I met her frigid gaze and furrowed my brow. People who *do* know me had said far worse things about me without it getting under my skin. And she wasn't entirely wrong, either, but for some reason the idea of her thinking so little of me without reason made me want to prove her wrong.

"This was a bad idea," she grabbed her purse off the bench at her side and stood, "I'm gonna go. Sorry for wasting your time."

Porter

"Sit down, Holly." The words came out as a command instead of a request, as I had meant them. She fell back into the booth and stared at me as if I had just pulled a gun on her.

"Stay," I forcibly softened my voice, "Have dinner with me. We're both adults here and I'd like to think we're both capable of making it through a single meal without maiming one another."

A cool mask of professionalism quickly replaced the look of surprise on her face. She calmly set her purse beside her and reached for her water cup, "Of course."

There was something about the way she held eye contact as she drank from the glass that unnerved me. She didn't even blink as her hazel eyes bore into mine; assessing, devouring, almost predatory.

Maybe I underestimated you, Holly Nash.

I returned the stare, feigning ignorance and doing my best to plaster a patient, unassuming look on my face. I wanted her to think I was just waiting for her to finish. I didn't want her to know that I was watching her swallow down the water and imagining that it was my dick sliding down her throat.

I could feel myself stiffen with each gulp she took and nearly cheered when she finally put the half-empty glass back on the table. I probably would have if her tongue hadn't darted out to clear her lips of any remaining fluid as she gasped for air. That quick flash of pink between her teeth sealed the deal she had no idea she had entered into with my libido.

"So you're just a nice person, trying to do the right thing. Righting a wrong and fighting social injustice one dinner date at a time. Who knew?"

I was ready for it that time and kept my guard up. I put on my best smile and shrugged my shoulders, trying for nonchalant, "I don't see why not."

She practically snorted in my face as she scoffed at the idea.

"I'll tell you why not, Porter. Guys like you," she pointed an accusing finger across the table at me, "you don't see others as *people*. You see them as objects. Just a tool to use as you see fit. Your entire career is a practicum in demeaning women and telling the public that it's perfectly acceptable to objectify us."

59

David Michael

Okay, that one caught me off guard.

"I didn't have you pegged as a feminist, Holly Nash. You didn't really strike me as the women-aren't-smart-enough-to-make-their-own-choices-and-the-only-reason-they-make-porn-is-because-men-make-them type. I will have you know that a lot of the women—not all of them, but many of them—do it because they *enjoy* it. Believe it or not, I *do* actually get to know my coworkers off set," *Sometimes* I added to myself, "If you think we bring these girls in at gun point and force them to do things they don't want to do, you've got another thing coming."

I lifted my own glass of water and took a swig as I waited for the tempest in her eyes to erupt.

"I didn't say you *force* them into doing anything, but let's be honest: The porn industry wouldn't exist if it weren't for men who would rather objectify women than actually get to know one as a person."

It was my turn to scoff in her face.

"You've got to be fucking kidding me!" I couldn't believe the words that had just come out of her mouth, "You don't think *I* get objectified? Are you high? Do you have *any* idea how many women pretend to be interested in Porter Hale only to be able to tell their friends that they fucked Ryder Ruff? You're really so blinded by your sex's struggle for equality that you don't think objectification happens on both sides of the fence? I knew there were some sheltered people in this world, Holly, but *that* is flirting dangerously with outright ignorance."

Her mask of professionalism had fallen away and there was something new, something careful and calculating, glinting deep in her eyes. I couldn't quite put my finger on it, but it wasn't sitting well with me.

"Let's get out your phone, Holly. I want you to go through your contacts list and find me *one* single woman between the ages of, let's say twenty and forty, who's never enjoyed porn or been to a strip club or ogled some shirtless fitness model on Facebook. Just one. If you can do that, I will acquiesce and admit that I stand corrected. One woman, Holly. Prove me wrong."

She seemed to be considering my offer as she stared at me. I could tell by the way she pressed her mouth into a fine line. She may as well have been chewing on her bottom lip. She finally tore her eyes away from mine and looked down at the table, quietly fidgeting with her fingernails.

"You're right," she practically whispered, "I apologize."

When she lifted her head again, the mask was back in place. She was cool and collected once more and took a quick sip of her water without making eye contact.

When Holly *did* meet my gaze again, her eyes had softened. She no longer exuded the holier-than-thou aura that had clung to her when she'd first sat down. She *almost* seemed comfortable to be sitting across the table from a porn star.

Almost.

"Shall we peruse the menu and flag down a waiter? I think we scared the poor kid off with our chosen topic of conversation. I busted him staring at my crotch when he took drink orders. I bet we get the bottle of wine I ordered for free," I winked at her as I picked up my menu, "Sometimes it pays to be a sex object."

Ten

Holly

The date had taken a turn for the strange and I wasn't sure how I felt about it.

Never in a million years had I expected to be lectured on objectification by a male porn star. Ever.

The weirdest part about the whole thing was that he was right.

And then for him to turn around and be completely okay with being objectified, by another man none-the-less, just blew every argument I had out of the water.

It's not every day Holly Nash gets talked into a corner.

Not only had he talked me there, I was kind of okay with staying there.

Porter Hale had a way with the words, once he was done berating me, which made it comfortable for me to let him take the lead. I could tell he was playing off my reactions and watching me like a hawk for the slightest response to his words, but that made it all the more captivating to me.

I had gone in blind and expected him to be a self-centered, egotistical prick. I had been pleasantly surprised when he actually made an effort to engage me in real conversation—something beyond shoptalk and the latest who's who.

I could feel my guard slipping more and more with each passing minute and I couldn't find it in me to care. He truly seemed like a genuine, *normal* guy.

Who just happened to have sex with beautiful women for a living.

Porter

He pushed the last bite of roasted duck into his mouth and sat back with a contented moan, "Delicious. The natural jus was the perfect touch."

And he's a foodie. Who would have thought?

"The Alaskan halibut was to die for as well," I glanced down at the half-eaten fish and wished there was more room in my stomach for it, "I should've skipped out on the tempura soft shell crab. I'm afraid I might rip a seam if I try to put anything else in my mouth."

There was a quick flush of red in his cheeks as the corners of his mouth quirked upward, but he schooled his expression quickly.

"Does that mean no dessert?"

I couldn't tell if he was joking or if he actually felt crushed by my inability to put anything else inside of me.

"By all means, help yourself! Surprisingly, I'm not in a rush to get out of here. I've really enjoyed your company tonight, Porter."

Something troubled flashed across his face for the briefest of moments before he cranked up the megawatt smile and picked up the dessert menu. I wasn't sure if I had imagined it or not, so I let it slide.

"These are all dude desserts," he complained, "I was hoping for something a little more feminine after dinner."

"What do you mean, 'dude desserts'?" I reached for the menu to see what he was talking about, "What did you have in mind?" My eyes quickly scanned the menu, judging the desserts fairly generic, before I looked back at him and froze.

"I was hoping for something along the lines of tiramisu," he reached forward and tenderly lifted my hand from the table, "it's so hard to find good lady fingers though." He placed a soft kiss on the very tip of my index finger, massaging the palm of my hand with his thumbs.

There were flashing red lights and sirens going off somewhere inside my head, but it felt like someone was holding a pillow over my brain and stifling my ability to reason.

"Exorcism!" I cried, yanking my hand back and picking up my purse.

The look of confusion on his face was both pathetic and comical all at once, but I couldn't risk being around him any longer. The leather seat was probably already soaked and I was convinced that my panties had climbed their way down my legs and rested somewhere around my ankles.

"Thank you for dinner, Porter," I said as I rose to my feet, "but I have to go now. I have a-" what did I have? "a thing."

Smooth.

I bolted before he even had a chance to say anything.

I slammed the door of my Audi and tore out of the parking lot like I had just planted a bomb in the women's bathroom. The two hundred and twenty horses under the hood carried me from zero to sixty in about seven seconds. It still wasn't fast enough. Nothing short of a jet engine could put enough space between Porter Hale and my unwieldy sex drive.

I could still feel my heart hammering in my chest as my brain recounted the way his lips had felt on my skin. The gentle brush of flesh on flesh had flooded my body with heat and sent my brain into short circuit mode. My face was flushed, my clothes felt too tight, and I was positive that my vagina would explode at any moment.

It wasn't until the red and blue lights flashed behind me and I heard the short quip of the police siren that my body came crashing down from the endorphin high I had been riding. I glanced down at the speedometer and swore as I put on my turn signal, let my foot off the gas pedal, and made my way over to the right hand shoulder of Wilshire Boulevard.

"Any idea how fast you were going, Miss?"

Sixty-eight.

"I'm not sure officer. I was just keeping up with the flow of traffic."

He raised an eyebrow at me and held out his hands for my license and registration. "What's the rush?"

My seventy-two year old grandmother fell down three flights of stairs and broke both hips.

"I'm running a bit late for a meeting downtown and let myself get carried away I guess."

Porter

"Stay put and turn off your car."

Fuck.

I drummed my fingers on the steering wheel and watched him as he climbed back into the driver's seat of his patrol car to run my registration.

With today's technology, I still can't figure out why the hell that part of the ticketing process always takes so damn long.

There's nothing worse than sitting on the side of the road with police lights flashing behind you and the rest of the world gawking like you're in a zoo. I always have the overwhelming urge to flip off the passers-by as they slow down to rubberneck. Not *every* arrest in Beverly Hills is an Olsen twin DUI, after all.

A massive black Land Rover pulled up along side me, travelling even slower than the rest of the cars that had passed, before pulling up against the curb in front of me.

"You've got to be fucking kidding me," I couldn't believe someone had actually stopped. If it was a paparazzi looking for his next breaking story I was going to lose my shit.

Then Porter Hale stepped out of the SUV and started toward my car.

There was a brief moment that I considered turning my car back on and gunning it. Vehicular Manslaughter is only a misdemeanor in most cases and, with a good lawyer, I probably wouldn't even get the maximum sentence of one year.

He walked right past my door and up to the police cruiser.

I watched the two of them in my side-view mirror as I crushed the steering wheel in an iron grip.

What the hell does he think he's doing?

I waited for the cop to just pull out his gun and shoot him, but it never happened. Instead, he got out of the cruiser laughing and shook the son-of-a-bitch's hand!

It took every ounce of my willpower to stay seated in my vehicle. I wanted to storm back there in punch Porter right in his big, dumb mouth.

The two of them walked back toward my car like old friends and I tried my best to school my features back into the late-but-innocent look of panic I had managed to pull off when handing over my paperwork.

The officer handed me my license and registration with barely a glance in my direction.

"You make sure to keep her behind you the rest of the way to that meeting, Mister Ruff. Try to keep it under the speed limit."

They shook hands and Porter thanked him with a megawatt smile that would have set my panties on fire in any other setting.

"I just saved you a five hundred dollar ticket," he said from the side of his mouth as he waved to the officer, "You're buying dinner next time."

Porter turned and walked back to his Land Rover without so much as a backward glance.

He waited for the cop to drive off before pulling away from the curb and accelerating through the intersection. He made a left two blocks down the road and disappeared from my sight.

I sat there in shocked silence and stared into the distance after him.

Not only had he managed to smooth talk his way into getting *me* out of a ticket, but he'd also managed to nail down a second date, if I wasn't mistaken.

That bastard was smooth.

I shot off a text message to Becks and turned the ignition.

I needed a drink.

I pulled into my driveway as she pulled up to the curb out front.

"I hate you," I spat before she had even closed the door to her Prius.

"I guess I don't need to ask how it went then," she said with a smile, "Let me guess; He came onto you and you flipped out and froze."

Exactly!

"No! It wasn't like that at all!"

"Yes it was," she countered confidently, "Now you want to drink about it and tell me all about how much you hate him when, really, he got under your skin and you're dying to see him again."

"I hate you."

Porter

I unlocked the front door and gestured Becks inside with a sweep of my arm.

She lifted herself onto the tips of her toes as she passed and planted a loud kiss on my cheek before bouncing off toward the kitchen.

I barely had time to drop my purse next to the couch and kick my stilettos off before she pounced on me like a starving lion. Wine in hand; she grilled me for every detail of my date with Porter.

I didn't spare her any of the details. Once my lips began to move, it was like I couldn't stop them. I could hear the words spilling from my mouth, but I had no control, even when they started bordering on pornographic as I described the way my body responded to his touch.

Becks hung on my every word with a faraway, dreamy look on her face. You'd think I was telling her a story about a princess finally meeting her Prince Charming instead of a sordid tale of a first date gone wrong.

Her eyes focused and her mouth dropped open in surprise when I got to the part about being pulled over and him riding in to save the day.

"Are you serious?" she asked, "He just strolled up to the cop and started talking to him? I figured he'd be a little bit full of himself, but that's a bit more brazen than even I thought he'd be!"

"The man is convinced that his penis can do anything! It's insane!"

Becks smiled into her glass as she took another sip of wine, "Have you *seen* that thing in action? I'm half-convinced his penis can do anything, too!"

I rolled my eyes at her and downed the rest of my wine in one massive gulp.

"No, Becks. I haven't seen it in action. To be honest, I don't really want to, either. It's bad enough he can look at me and set my panties on fire. I don't need to make it even worse by giving my imagination some gasoline to toss on the flames."

She lifted the bottle from the coffee table and refilled our glasses before saying, "I promise you, Holly. Whatever your imagination tells you about his prowess, it doesn't compare. Not even close."

"I don't care, Rebecca. Stop talking about it and drink your wine."

"You're doing yourself a disservice," she muttered into her merlot.

I huffed out an irritated sigh before shifting the focus *away* from Porter's thrusting hips and silver tongue.

"What the hell did you and Mitch end up doing after you beat me to death with The Kit?"

"Mitch had a date, so he took off and I just went home," she leaned back against the arm of the couch and tucked her bare feet under my leg, "I was about three seconds away from attacking a pint of ice cream with a spoon when you called. My hips thank you for your timing."

"Oh, please," I lowered my brow and pinned her with a no-bullshit stare, "You could lie on your back under a soft-serve machine for an hour and not gain a pound. A pint of ice cream would probably do you some good, you skinny little twig."

"You know how it is in this town better than anyone, Holly. Until I either marry Johnny Depp, or land myself a Meryl Streep-level role, I've gotta keep this waist as tiny as I possibly can. Casting directors don't put whales in leading roles."

"We did in Free Willy," I had to raise my glass to hide my grin "besides, Hollywood has become less about the glitz and the glamour and more about the actual acting."

"You're full of shit. That may be true when it comes to the actual audition, but nobody gets in that door until *you* decide they *look* the part."

This was a conversation we'd had dozens of times before and it had a way of getting heated pretty quickly. I was half tempted to go back to talking about Porter just to avoid the fight.

"Becks, we both know that making it big in this shit show is like winning the lottery. The only way to make it is to keep playing the game and hope that, eventually, someone takes notice."

"I know," she agreed, "it's just a pain in my ass. I'm *really* tired of being the dumb girl in b-line horror flicks."

Porter

"But you're *so* good at it, honey!" I teased, "Your death scenes are always spectacular!"

"My death scenes are always CGI."

I burst out laughing before I could stop myself. The way she had said it just struck a chord with me and I couldn't help it. It was probably the wine. Luckily, it appeared to be doing its job with her, too. She added her quiet giggles to my own unrestrained laughter.

I swiped at the tears of laughter that had begun to form on my lashes and took a few deep breaths while I attempted to gather myself.

"So who's the flavor of the week that has caught Mitch's attention?" I knew my best friend wouldn't have let him out of her sight without a proper "interview", as she called them. The rest of us called them inquisitions.

"Some bartender he met on one of those gross dating apps. I'm willing to bet the guy just wants to hook up and never talk to him again. I keep telling him that the internet is *not* the way to meet guys, but he just doesn't listen. One of these days he's going to get chopped up into little tiny pieces and dumped in the ocean. There are some psychos out there, Holly. Like, Norman Bates status."

Becks was our resident pessimist when it came to relationships. Nobody doubted that she would be the last man standing when it came time to take the trip to the altar.

She had gone buck-wild in our college days. The girl had been in more laps than a napkin. Unfortunately, she wasn't the type to think with her hormones. She always got her heart involved and I watched it break every time a one-night-stand never called her back.

When we graduated, she jumped on the chastity bandwagon and turned into a bit of a cynic. She dated, but never anything serious and, to my knowledge, never slept with any of them no matter how many dates they took her on. It was like she was testing them without letting them know that there were rules to follow. It was a game that her poor guys never even knew they were playing. Each time one of them got tired of her pulling away, she became more resolute in her belief than men are scum.

I never could figure out what she expected from them and I knew better than to ask. I always just assumed that she loved the thrill of being chased, but had no desire to actually let one catch her.

"Earth to Holly!" Becks snapped her fingers in front of my face, pulling my gaze from the swirling red of my wine.

"Huh?"

"You zoned out on me. Do you even know what I was talking about?"

"Um, yeah," I shook my head, "You were talking about Mitch's date."

"I was, yes. Ages ago. Did you miss my whole diatribe about Ryder's money shots?"

"Porter," I corrected automatically, "And yes, apparently. I can't say I'm all that upset about it either. I don't want to talk about the Clit Wizard anymore. I've already decided that I'm not seeing him again. There's no way we'd work out, Becks."

"You don't know that!" she protested.

"Oh, but I do," I said coolly, "We're just too different. No amount of chemistry can bridge that gap."

"You're just determined to suck all the fun out of my life, aren't you?"

"Yes, Becks. My sole purpose in life is to *not* date a porn star just so you miss out on all the dirty details. If you like him so much, *you* go date him!"

Her mouth snapped shut as she seemed to consider my proposition for a moment.

"You're not dating him either, Becks! I don't want him in my life! I don't want to be around him at all! He's a *porn star* for Christ's sake! There is *nothing* outside of sex and money that he can possibly offer me!"

My best friend's eyes narrowed. She stared at me long and hard before she spoke quietly, "When did you become so judgmental, Holly? When did stereotypes become an option for you?"

It was my turn to be struck speechless.

Porter

She stared at me silently for several long moments, waiting for my response.

After the silence stretched well into uncomfortable territory, I whispered the only words that came to mind, "I don't know."

Eleven
Porter

"Honestly, Preston, I don't know why I even try! The woman hates me. There is no coming back from this. It's a lost cause."

"Nobody can hate you, Porter. You're too damn charismatic for your own good. It's literally impossible."

"Well, Holly Nash does."

I had just finished giving him the details of my miserable dinner with the beast of Hollywood. I tossed back another shot of Jack and let the burn of the alcohol chase away the last remaining traces of Holly's gentle smile and steely, sensual gaze.

"Why do you care so much?"

"Because she's my ticket out, Preston."

It was only a half-lie.

And Preston knew it. He grinned at me over his martini.

"There are dozens of other casting directors you could sleep with to get your big break, Porter."

"But none of them are Holly Nash."

The weight of the statement packed a hell of a punch with me.

I told myself that my newfound infatuation with her was just because I wasn't accustomed to being denied. It was sound logic according to my ego, but part of me was screaming "Bullshit!"

I did my best to school my features so that he didn't pick up on it. If Preston thought for even an instant that there was something more to my feelings for Holly, he'd turn into a dog with a bone.

That bone wasn't one I was ready to chew on just yet.

Porter

"She's the best, little brother." I reached around the bar and grabbed the bottle of Blue Label Johnny Walker that he always kept stashed out of sight. I poured a neat two fingers and raised my glass, "You know how I feel about the best."

He rolled his eyes and raised his own glass. "When you can have anything you want," he lowered his voice and did his best imitation of me, "why settle for less than the best?"

It had been my mantra for more than a decade. My father had asked me that very question once when I was nine and trying to decide on a birthday present. It just stuck.

We sipped our drinks and settled into a comfortable silence.

After several long seconds and another sip of scotch, he set his glass down with a gentle clink and leaned his elbows on the gleaming bar top.

"Cut the shit, Porter. You like her."

The little shit was sharp. I didn't insult him by denying it.

"You can try to pretend it's just business all you want, but I'm not stupid. I've known you better than you know yourself. I've never seen you like this over a woman, regardless of her job title. There's a hell of a lot more to this than you're telling me. I'm gonna guess there's a hell of a lot more to it than you're willing to admit to yourself, too. But I'll tell you this, if there's *anything* going on between the two of you, it's worth pursuing. Women like her don't come along every day."

I downed the rest of my Johnny in a single gulp.

"It's been nice chatting with you, baby brother, but I have shit to do. Say a word about any of this to Holly and I'll kick your ass."

I walked out of my Preston's house without another word or a backward glance. There were a lot of things I'd talk to the kid about, but my infatuation with his friend was *not* one of them. He was reliable in a lot of ways, but keeping secrets for me had never really been one of his strong suits.

Especially where women were concerned.

I climbed inside my Land Rover and slammed my finger down on the ignition button. The engine and the stereo roared to life in unison, the soothing sounds of Metallica's '*Fuel*' came blaring out of the speakers. There was no room left in my head for Preston's words to echo around and for this, I was thankful.

I slammed my foot down on the gas pedal, shooting gravel behind me in an impressive spray of tiny projectiles.

I shot onto the street and made a right. I wasn't sure where I was going, or what I'd do when I got there, but it seemed that my foot was in a hurry to arrive.

I found myself flying south on the Five a few minutes later.

The windows were rolled down, the music was cranked up, and the faintest hint of the Pacific hung in the summer air. Only the occasional passing car and the glow of streetlights at regular intervals punctuated the rolling darkness of the freeway in front of me.

It was just after four in the morning when I crossed into San Diego city limits. I headed southwest on Camino Del Rio and continued toward the beach on Rosecrans. Ten minutes later, I parked the Rover at the edge of the sand and changed into my board shorts.

There was no need to bother with the awkward hassle of changing inside the car. Even if there was anyone else around at four-thirty in the morning, it was hard to find someone in the state of California who didn't know my name. If they didn't recognize my face, there were other parts of my anatomy that tended to get me out of trouble.

The sand was still warm as I stepped onto it. Each tiny granule scrubbed at my feet with every step and the crash of the waves to my left took me away from the city as I walked north along the coast.

There's something about the beaches of southern California that just draws me to them like a moth to a flame. I know that hundreds, if not thousands, of deadly creatures live beneath the thunderous surf, but I'll be damned if I can keep myself out of the ocean. Some people are drawn to the mountains, some to the forest, and some of the most fucked up people I know are actually drawn to the flat no-mans-land of the Bible Belt. I am not one of those people. I *have* to be close to the ocean. It's like a giant, wet security blanket full of killer beasts.

Porter

The sun had come up when I finally pulled myself from the hypnotic pull of the ocean to take stock of my surroundings. A few hundred yards further north, the coastline rose sharply out of the sea to form a small range of cliffs.

I had kayaked them dozens of times.

One of the main attractions of La Jolla were the caverns that wormed through the rock faces at low tide. The first of the adventure seekers were already packing their boats into the water.

I found myself walking toward the kayak rental kiosk up the shore a ways to join them when my phone rang.

"Yeah?"

"Where the hell are you, Ryder?"

My manager, Ryan, sounded pissed.

"Um, in La Jolla about to hit the caves. Why?"

"You were supposed to be on set twenty minutes ago, dude! What the fuck are you doing in La Jolla?"

"Fuck!" I yelled, startling a few nearby kayak-toting passers-by, "I spaced it! I drove down to San Diego early this morning and just started walking. I needed to clear my head."

"You're telling me you walked all the way to La Jolla and your fucking car is in San Diego?"

"Yeah," I knew the conversation wasn't going to end well.

"Don't move a fucking inch. I'm sending a car to the cliffs."

The line went dead in my ear and I sighed; So much for a relaxing day off.

As I waited for the car to show up, I watched as dozens of boats, most of them single occupancy, marched passed me in a colorful line of buoyant Kevlar and plastic. I felt a tinge of jealousy over the fun they were all going to have without me.

Not to mention the workout.

Even at low tide, some of the waves could get a little choppy and raise the water level in the caverns to the point where you had to lay back to avoid hitting your head on the ceiling. That also meant you had to fight the ebb and flow in both directions to keep from being swept out to sea, capsized, or shoved into the darkest arms of the massive cave structure.

75

It hadn't even been ten minutes when a black sedan skidded to a stop at the edge of the sand and blasted its horn. Ryan must've threatened the poor dude within inches of his life to get someone out there so fast.

The driver stepped out of the car looking a little frazzled as I approached and opened the back door for me.

"You don't mind if I sit up front with you, do you?"

"N-n-n-o sir!" he stammered, "Not at all!"

The door he held open slammed shut with a bang and he ran around the front of the car to open the passenger side door.

"Thanks, boss," I smiled.

After I was carefully secured in the passenger seat, he jumped back behind the wheel and glanced at the clock on the dashboard. I heard him curse quietly under his breath as he slammed the car into reverse and pounded the accelerator to the floor.

We spun ninety degrees in the small parking lot and took off like a shot. I didn't even see him put it in drive. The dude had to be a stunt driver or something.

After a harrowing 50-minute drive back into Los Angeles, we skidded to a halt outside a massive warehouse covered in corrugated siding.

He glanced down at the clock once more and let out a long, relieved sigh.

"Was it a threat or a bribe?" I asked, knowing all too well that Ryan knew how to light a fire under a person's ass.

The driver grinned at me but avoided eye contact, "Bribe."

"Damn. I was betting on threat. The mood he was in when I talked to him was working against you."

The driver smiled, but didn't say anything as he nervously ran his hands over the steering wheel.

"Well, did you make it in time?"

He nodded his head, "Barely."

"Good," I smiled at him, "Anything I can do to get you to stick around for a few hours and drive me back to San Diego after the shoot?"

Porter

His face turned a brilliant color of red as his hands tightened on the black leather of the wheel in front of him. I knew the telltale signs of a fanboy moment when I saw them and braced myself.

I've heard everything from "Can I have an autograph?" to "Can I suck you off?", so I always get a little bit nervous when those situations arise.

I was *not* expecting what came out of his mouth.

"Can I come sit on set with you?"

After a moment of confused silence, I got my shit together and shrugged my shoulders, "Sure! I mean, it'll probably be boring as hell for you, but I can make that happen."

We got out of the car together and headed for the tiny steel entrance next to the sealed jumbo-sized bay door.

"Just stay with me and play along."

He nodded his understanding and we entered the rabbit hole.

"What's your name?" I whispered?

"Brandon," he hissed back.

"Brandon!" I yelled as we walked toward the dressing rooms, "I'm gonna need some coffee! Like, ten minutes ago! Get your ass moving!"

He stood frozen for a moment before catching on and scurrying off to find me what I had asked for.

I had yelled in order to draw the attention of everyone on set and establish him as my personal assistant. Everyone had seen his face and wouldn't question his presence for the rest of the day. My end of the bargain had turned out to be unfairly easy to hold up.

"Ryder!" I could only assume the man stomping toward me from the other side of the set was Ken Farren, the director. I'd never worked with him before, so I wasn't sure what to expect. My name alone carried enough weight that I knew I didn't have a whole lot to worry about, but he definitely looked pissed off enough to try something stupid.

"Ken!" I greeted him with a disarming smile, "Sorry I'm late! I had some personal errands to run and they took a bit longer than expected."

David Michael

"Cut the shit you self-absorbed little prick," he jammed a finger into the center of my chest, "Going on a bender and waking up too hung-over to function isn't something I would call an errand. I've heard all about you and your brothers. I know that you're all pains in the ass to work with. You think that the world revolves around you because your father was a legend. Well I've got some fucking news for you, kid! These people?" he swung his arm wildly to indicate the rest of the crew, "*they* all have shit to do, too. Instead, they've been sitting here for the last two fucking hours waiting for you to sober up and decide to come to work."

My fists were clenched at my sides so tightly that my nails were digging into my palms. I clamped my teeth down on my cheek to keep myself from saying anything I'd regret. The metallic taste of blood told me that I needed to get away from the guy before I lost my shit *and* my job.

With a concentrated effort, I unclenched my fists and tried to speak as calmly as possible, "I'm here now. Where's the dressing room?" The words came out as more of a snarl than I had intended, but I didn't spit in his face or break his nose, so I decided to call it a win.

He pointed to a room to my right that was barely more than a closet, "Be on set in *two* minutes."

Brandon returned with a steaming cup of coffee as Ken spun to return to set. The director snatched it from his hand and threw it in his face as he screamed, "He doesn't deserve any fucking coffee!"

Brandon stood there in shock as the hot liquid streamed down his face.

I motioned for him to follow me into the dressing room and slammed the door behind us.

My clothes were off in record time, even for me. I thrust them in his face, barely remembering not to throw them at him, "Here. They might be a little bit tight, but at least they're not covered in fucking coffee. I can't believe that prick!"

He stood there staring at me with his eyes and mouth wide open for a moment before he seemed to realize he was making it weird.

"Thanks," he muttered as he took the swim trunks and tee shirt from my hand.

I had to give him credit; he only glanced down at my junk once.

I nodded at him and turned to the chair that had my outfit for the shoot draped over it. "Sometimes I hate this job," I confided, "I think costume designers are just jealous bastards who like to torture those of us who have to wear the stuff they come up with."

I stuffed my legs into the black leather pants and began the slow process of pulling them up.

My cock was going to look like a damn nightstick in the fucking things.

Brandon turned around in a show of modesty that I wasn't accustomed to. He stripped off the black slacks and black button up he'd been wearing and quickly stepped into the board shorts I had given him. It had been a *long* time since someone had made me feel like we were in a junior high locker room and I couldn't help but laugh.

"What?" he spun around and flushed a brilliant red.

"Nothing," I tried to control the chuckles that kept jumping out of me, "I'm just not used to modesty is all. In this industry, everyone just walks around with their cocks swinging freely in your face. It was refreshing, I suppose."

"Oh," he smiled sheepishly as I finally pulled the leather over my hips and tucked my package inside, "I don't get naked in front of many people, let alone dudes. Not to mention you're the biggest porn star in the world. It's... intimidating."

"First rule of Porn Club, Brandon:" I chuckled at my own joke, "You've got the biggest cock in the room. Even if you have a pencil dick, you act like it's something Godzilla would be proud to call his own."

"What?" confusion and shock washed over his face, "Porn club? What are you talking about?"

"If you're gonna make it in this industry, that's the mentality you have to have. I assume that's why you wanted to be on set today, right? A foot in the door?"

"No!" I was growing accustomed to the nice shade of maroon his face could turn in an instant, "I wanted to be here because you're shooting with Chardonnay Hilton! I own every film she's ever done and it's a once-in-a-lifetime opportunity for me to see her perform live!"

Well that's a first...

I was still staring at him in surprise when a bang like a gunshot sounded at the door, "Your two minutes are up! Get your ass out here and do your fucking job!"

Brandon raised an eyebrow, "Are all porn directors like that asshole?"

I threw an arm over his shoulder and led him to the door, "Not all of them. He's an exceptionally irritating case of asshole, even for this industry."

Another series of loud bangs filled the room, spiking my blood pressure and causing us both to jump.

I ripped the door open with such force that Ken stumbled backwards several steps in surprise.

I held up my left hand to Brandon, "Help me get into this stupid thing?"

Dangling from my fingertips was a leather shoulder harness. Two-inch strips of black leather, studded with metal rivets formed the straps that would go over my shoulders. They were attached in a figure-eight formation by a stainless steel D-ring that would sit right between my shoulder blades. The contraption would force my shoulders back, highlighting my pecs for the camera, and the leather would be pulled tight enough to dig into my shoulders a little bit and make my already large biceps look absolutely massive.

Shoulder gear had always been a plus in my book. Leather was one of the few things from work that I was willing to take into the privacy of my own bedroom. I was just glad that I didn't get paid to wear the pants for very long. They were already starting to chafe.

Brandon made a show of helping me into the harness that I very clearly could have gotten into myself, and followed a few steps behind me as I made my way to the set.

80

Porter

A massive four-poster bed loomed in the center of the room. The frame had been painted a matte black as well as the backdrop and floor. A shockingly vibrant splash of red silk covered the mattress and box spring. Sprawled in the center of the sea of strawberry-colored bedding was a redhead with a delicate frame, loose flowing hair, and milky-white skin for days. Her patent leather stilettos were the same color as the sheets and so was her corset.

Even her lips popped with the color.

All I could think about was how much of a bitch it would be to wash that lipstick off my junk after the shoot was finished.

"She's even more perfect in person," Brandon whispered from my side.

"Just stay quiet and keep out of everyone's way," I advised, "Assistant or no, you get in the way, they *will* make you leave. If you have to, find a dark corner and rub one out. You might have to fight a camera guy for it though. You've been warned."

We parted ways at the toy rack.

After a cursory glance, I could tell we'd probably only end up using three or four of the two-dozen props they had brought in. My bets were on the dildo, the butt plug, the riding crop, and, God willing, the ball gag.

Chardonnay and I exchanged brief introductions. It was just enough for me to decide that she was a frosty bitch both on and off the set. I wasn't sure who I was less excited about working with for the next three hours, her or the psychotic director.

"Now that our leading man has overcome his drinking problem, let's get this show on the road!"

I nearly ripped the megaphone out of Ken's hand and stuffed it down his throat.

The crew sprang into action as lights were repositioned and run through their different settings. Filters were changed out, seemingly at Ken's whim, brightness was adjusted, some lights were even swapped out entirely only to be changed back to where they'd been when they started.

For someone who was so pissed off that I wasn't on set on time, there sure seemed to be a lot of shit left to do before we could start shooting.

My costar huffed out a long, bored breath beside me.

"Has he been like this all morning?"

"Yep," she confirmed, "at least he's not throwing things anymore. He really doesn't like you or your brothers very much."

I shrugged my shoulders nonchalantly, causing the leather to strain against my bulk, "There are a lot of people who don't like my family. The Westboro Baptists picketed our house once. Now *that's* a special brand of stupid right there."

She laughed quietly, showing the first sign that she wasn't an absolute ice queen, "I worked with Parker once. He told me the story. Did they really stand out there for two days with signs and yell at you guys every time you came out of the house?"

"Yup. Poor Preston was only about six at the time. He didn't understand what the hell was going on. He had snuck out to play and they yelled and screamed at him until he ran back into the house in tears. My mom had to lock me in the bathroom to keep me from going out there and doing something stupid. My dad was off on some shoot, of course, so I felt like it was my job, as the man of the house, to make them leave."

"Did Parker really shoot off a shotgun to get them to leave?"

It was my turn to laugh.

"No," I smiled, "I'm surprised he told you that version instead of the one where he lobbed a beehive into the middle of them. That's always been his favorite. Unfortunately, the real story is a bit mundane. We just stayed inside for so long that they got bored and went away. If you go to their website, I think there's still a page where they brag about the two-day stand they took against moral corruption outside the Ruff House. Those people are whack jobs."

"If you two are done," the megaphone screeched, "you have paychecks to earn."

"I'm gonna kill him before this is through," I growled to her through gritted teeth.

Porter

"Not if I beat you to it," she chirped. The million-dollar smile on her face could've fooled even me.

At least I finally got to work with someone with some acting skills!

Unfortunately, it turned out that her only real ability was smiling.

Staging was tedious at best. Blocking was like trying to teach a cat to play dead. The girl just didn't get it. Luckily, the script wasn't too complicated. She only had to have her lines read back to her a dozen times each.

Ken had blown through an entire pack of cigarettes before the cameras even started rolling.

"Clear the set!" he screamed into his microphone.

Finally, it was time to start shooting.

I made my way over to the fluffer. She was probably in her early twenties. Mid-length brunette hair, too much eye makeup, and a tan so dark you could tell she spent at least four days a week in a tanning bed. Her eye shadow was silver over her greyish-green eyes and her lipstick, as she took my cock in her mouth, was Barbie pink.

I let my head fall back and stared up into the darkness of the rafters over head while she did her business.

Ken called Chardonnay back on scene and that was my cue. I retrieved my now-stiff anatomy from the pearly-pink clutches of Hooker Barbie and did my best to tuck it back into the tight leather.

It looked like I had a nine and a half inch club vacuum-sealed to my leg.

I shook my head over the cheesy representation of BDSM and walked into frame.

"It's *my* fantasy, right?" Chardonnay asked in a low, smoky voice, "That means I can make you do whatever I want, right?"

I crossed my arms in front of me causing my biceps to bulge and strain against the harness and my pecs to swell into massive pads of muscle. I just nodded my head slowly in response to her question.

She reached over to the wall of toys that had been wheeled next to the bed, "I wanna start with this one."

David Michael

She grabbed the flogger off the rack and slapped it gently against her palm. It was black leather, about eighteen inches in total length, with dozens of strips that, if used properly, could leave tiny little welts without causing any actual damage.

I held out my hand and waited for her to place the handle in my palm.

Instead of doing what had been blocked out, she shook her head and bit her bottom lip. She ran the handle of it between her legs and curled a finger at me, motioning for me to join her on the bed.

Knowing that sometimes you just had to go with your gut, I chose to follow her lead. Ken hadn't called cut yet, so I didn't really have much choice.

The moment my hands and knees hit the mattress, she sprang on me like a tiger, bringing the business end of the flogger down on my lower back and ass.

"That's for keeping me waiting," she moaned as I grunted in surprise. I pressed her down on her back and bit her collarbone. She brought the leather straps down once again, causing my hips to jerk forward and rub my leather-clad cock against her thigh. "That one was just for fun," she whispered in my ear.

So that's *how you wanna play it, huh?*

I grabbed her wrist the next time she lifted her arm and stopped its descent before she could make contact again. I pried the hard leather handle from her palm and threw the thing across the room.

It was my turn to play.

I reached over to the wall of toys and drew a four-foot strand of satin into the bed with us. She smiled pretty for the camera before closing her eyes and lifting her head to be blindfolded.

Instead, I jerked her arms above her and quickly tied them to the bed.

"The best part of a fantasy," I growled against her neck, "is how quickly it can become reality."

Her body arched beneath me, thrusting her tits into my chest and her hips into my groin.

Porter

I made a meal out of her, nipping, licking, and kissing my way over her mostly-exposed breasts. I left the corset in place, but quickly unsnapped the garter belts attached to her panties and rolled the thigh-high socks down to the ends of her toes, massaging her long, firm legs as I went.

She squirmed with each flick of my tongue as I made my way back up to the inside of her thighs.

She let out a pealing squeal of pleasure and ground her mound against my face the first time I thrust my tongue inside of her.

That just wouldn't do.

I grabbed the ball gag from the rack and quickly secured the metal clasp at the back of her head before flipping her over so that she was forced to support her weight with her elbows and her knees. The satin had twisted with her, drawing her hands tighter to the metal frame.

I lay down on my back with my head between her legs. She was smooth and swollen as I sucked her clit into my mouth. I applied pressure to it with my lips as I quickly flicked my tongue back and forth. She moaned against the rubber ball in her mouth and squeezed my face with her thighs.

I reached down and quickly freed my dick from the crushing pressure of the leather pants. It sprang into my hand like a lightsaber to a Jedi and I began a slow, gentle rhythm that would look good for the camera without taking me too close to the edge.

I focused on the technicalities of what I was doing. I did my best to be mindful of camera angles, lighting problems, and the fact that we needed to get a good forty-five minutes of footage out of the shoot before we could go. I also tried my hardest to ignore the camera guy with the raging hard-on practically on top of my left hand.

I slid my limb away from the offending bulge and slipped two fingers into Chardonnay. Her body jolted at the sudden intrusion and her slick entrance clamped down around the digits, crushing them in its warmth. The muscles slowly loosened up as I twisted my wrist and slowly pulled out of her while still working her with my mouth.

David Michael

Another twist of the wrist and I plunged my fingers back inside her. Her body rocked backward to meet me this time and we quickly fell into a gentle rhythm.

The next time she tightened around my fingers it was accompanied by a moan as her orgasm trickled down my wrist. I continued working both of our sexes with my hands and lapped at her slit with my tongue as she rode out the wave of her first climax.

When the pulsing around my fingers finally subsided and her entire body shuddered above me, I finally slid them out of her and rose behind her with my cock still in my hand.

I used my free hand to pull my next toy off the rack and smiled when her eyes sparked with desire.

It was a riding crop about the length of my forearm. The handle fit comfortably in my palm. The two-inch keeper at the other end of the fiberglass rod was a soft and flexible strip of leather.

I flicked her hair out of the way and pressed the cool leather to her cheek, "I don't remember telling you to come."

I freed my other hand and used it to unlace the corset she was still cinched into. Once the back fell open and the lace and bone contraption fell to the bed, I slowly trailed the crop down her neck and spine.

When I reached the mounds of her now-bare ass, I lifted the crop several inches and brought it down on her with a snap. Not hard enough to cause any real pain, but enough to leave a pink spot and a bit of a sting.

I did the same thing on the other cheek.

I placed the crop on the bed next to us and made a show of surveying the rack for my next tool. I already knew which one was going in her next, but we had a job to do and it all had to look good on camera.

I took the medium sized butt plug in my hand and held it up thoughtfully. Her eyes had followed me like a hawk and I saw the smile play around the ball gag when I reached for the lube.

I could see why Brandon had been so excited to watch her work. It's not very often you come across a porn star who genuinely *enjoys* their job—especially not the women.

Porter

I pressed the slippery toy to her hole and made it appear as if I was pressing it inside of her. In reality, I was letting her press her body backwards onto the point so that it slid in at her pace. It vanished inch-by-inch until it was seated inside of her and only the broad, flat base was visible.

I quickly pulled a vibrator off the shelf, lubed it up, and flashed her a wicked smile. I drove it into her without warning and my dick gave a quick jump of approval at the gasp of surprise that escaped her.

I flicked the switch on the bottom and the thing buzzed to life. I drove it into her again and again, knowing that it wouldn't be long before she came. She threw her head back, causing her hair to tumble down the perfect curve of her spine. I felt her body tighten around the vibrating latex and she screamed against the rubber gag in her mouth.

I removed the vibrator in one quick motion, causing her to moan sadly at the lack of sensation.

I retrieved the crop from its position next to my knee and brought it down on her ass once more, harder than the last time.

She jumped and moaned as her ass tightened around the plug.

"That's twice without permission," I brought the leather-tipped rod down across her ass again, "Why is it so hard to find someone who learns from their mistakes in this city?"

The crop came down once more with a snap before I discarded it on the floor next to the bed.

A stagehand scurried through the shadows to retrieve it then vanished back into the darkness without a sound.

I took my position between her thighs and put the head of my shaft against her slit. Each time she tried to back up onto me, I pulled away just enough to keep myself from entering her. I did this until she had backed up so far that her arms were completely stretched out above her head.

Then I leaned forward, still careful not to push inside of her, and rolled each of her nipples between my thumb and forefinger. They stiffened at my touch and she all but pulled her arms out of their sockets in an effort to get me inside her.

David Michael

I held my hand out for a condom and the same stagehand that had scampered off with the crop dropped one into my palm.

I quickly rolled it on, knowing that the process would be edited out of the final product, and returned my hands to her breasts.

I continued to tease the tiny nubs at their peaks with my fingertips and slid the length of my shaft along her slit. She was so hot that I could feel her heat blowing onto me like a furnace through the condom.

I lowered my left hand to rub quick circles over her clit. She came fast and hard.

I drove myself into her as she rode that high. Buried to the hilt, I sat still and waited for her to finish. Her entire body convulsed with the power of her climax this time and I couldn't help but take pride in my ability to get her off.

When her body finished shaking, I began to sharply piston my hips into her. I could feel the rubber plug rubbing along the top of my shaft and wondered briefly what it felt like for her.

I slipped my fingers under the strap of the gag at the back of her head and jerked it backwards, "You enjoy being punished, don't you?" I snarled. I slammed my hips against her ass, driving the plug and my cock even deeper inside of her. She whimpered in response, but the gleam in her eye and the way her body responded to mine told me that she loved every minute of it.

I performed my end of our job spectacularly, making her erupt in fits of ecstasy again and again. She made sure to up the dramatics for the cameras and the director and crew stayed quiet. We both knew how to work it and they knew it.

After her sixth orgasm since the shoot began, I pulled out of her and yanked off the condom with a snap. I'd go all day with one of those damn things in the way. I took matters into my own hands and quickly worked myself to a climax of my own.

As the hot spray of my own orgasm landed across the base of the plug and up her back, she wiggled her ass and moaned. After the heady high of a good orgasm finally cleared, I reached down and slowly removed the plug, discarding it on the floor the same way I had the riding crop.

Porter

I brought my open palm down on her flushed ass cheek.

"Maybe next time you'll remember who's in charge."

I walked off set without another word and bee-lined it for the bathroom.

I could hear the chatter of the crew outside the door as they began to wrap up. The whirr of power tools joined the cacophony as they began to tear down the set. I heard Chardonnay's voice as she passed the door but couldn't quite tell what she was saying. I didn't care enough to go find out either.

Moments later, there was a sharp knock on the door and I remembered my "assistant" that I had left on set. Hopefully he had brought me my clothes that I'd left in the closet of a dressing room.

"It's open!" I called.

When the door swung open, I was surprised to see Ken standing behind me in the mirror.

"What can I do for you, Ken?"

"Nothing," he replied, trying to sound casual, "I just thought I'd pop in."

He seemed sheepish.

"You thought you'd pop in? While I wash my dick in a bathroom sink?"

The man blushed. That was the moment I knew I'd seen it all. A porn director had just blushed like a schoolgirl right before my very eyes.

"N-n-n-no," he stammered and gently closed the door behind him, "I guess I just wanted to apologize. I was an asshole when you got here. After seeing the magic you just worked out there, I can promise you it would have been worth waiting another twelve hours. The things I said earlier were uncalled for. You've got talent, kid."

He left the room without another word. I just stood there, stunned, with my dick in my hand and the water still running in the sink.

The sound of water hitting the floor pulled me back to reality and I quickly shut off the faucet to stem the flood.

I scrubbed the leftover lube off my hands and groin and was about to make my way back to the dressing room to get out of the damn harness and into my own clothes when there was another knock on the door.

I pulled it open and Brandon stood there with my board shorts, tee shirt, and flip-flops in his hands.

He was decked out in a brand new pair of Diesel jeans and an Affliction tee.

"Where'd the new duds come from?" I asked as I stepped into my shorts.

"The director felt bad for giving me a coffee shower, so he sent someone from wardrobe out shopping during the shoot. You guys kinda kicked ass from what I gather, so everyone pretty much stood around with nothing to do."

"He also realized that if he ever wanted me to work with him again, he had some ass-kissing to do," I clarified as I slipped into my sandals, "Let's blow this joint and get me back to my car."

We walked companionably back to his black sedan where, out of habit, he opened the back door for me.

Instead of insisting that I ride in the front seat with him, I dropped into the back seat and sprawled out. I wasn't in the mood for idle chitchat and that late in the afternoon; it was going to be a *long* drive through L.A. traffic.

I needed a power nap.

Twelve
Holly

Becks' words had been ringing around in my head for days: "When did you become so judgmental, Holly?"

She didn't think anything of it, but I had been carrying that single question around with me like a hookworm. It had been nearly a week since my failed dinner with Porter and I was beginning to go crazy.

It didn't make me a bad person to have standards, right? I mean, Porter Hale has more money than Donald Trump, more friends than Oprah, and a sex drive comparable to Ron Jeremy, but we had *nothing* in common. We couldn't even get through a simple meal together without drama.

We'll ignore the fact that my body and my brain had disagreed on how to approach the situation, causing said drama.

It just wouldn't work. Plain and simple.

There was a soft knock at the door of my office and I looked up to see Mitch's head poking around the corner.

"You busy?"

"No," I sighed, "What's up?"

I beckoned for him to come in and he closed the door behind him.

"What the hell is wrong with you Holly Nash?" He plopped down in the chair across from my desk and draped his legs over one arm. "You've been moping around this place like an abused puppy for a week now. I can't take it anymore. It's almost like you're," he waved his hand in circles as if trying to conjure the right word, "agreeable. I don't like it. It's freaking me out."

I was thinking about how much of the story to leave out when he caught my gaze and said, "Don't even think about bullshitting me."

I blew out a frustrated breath and dove in headfirst.

"My date, if you can call it that, with Porter last week was a total failure. The man is simply impossible to talk to. We have nothing in common and I spent the entire time uncomfortable. It was awkward."

And my vagina wanted to eat him alive.

"So I called Becks on my way home and made her meet me at the house for drinks. You know how she gets when she drinks," I paused so he could nod his understanding, "Anyway, she started spouting off about Porter and I and somehow managed to get it in her head that I'm judgmental and that I have painted Porter as a stereotypical porn star."

"*My* Holly Nash? Judgmental?"

"Exactly!" I cried, thrilled that someone was finally on my side, "I'm *so* not judgmental!"

"Holly," he swung his legs forward and leaned over to place his elbows on his knees, "I don't send anyone into your office if they have blonde hair or weigh less than one-fifty. Why? Because I know it's a waste of time. It doesn't matter *how* much talent they have or *how* impressive their résumé is, you will either send them out of here in tears, or never send them on a single audition. Now, I don't know what you have against skinny bitches and blondes, but it's there and it's real. You judge every person who walks through that door before they even have a chance to open their mouths."

I opened my mouth to defend myself, but he held up his hands and continued before I could get a word in.

"I'm not saying it's a bad thing, honey. We all do it. I think you'd be amazed at how many people I turn away as soon as they walk in the door. In this industry, the ability to judge someone in a few moments is paramount and you know it. What you *haven't* seemed to master yet, is how to turn that shit off when you leave the office. If you keep turning people away because they're wearing the wrong brand of jeans that day, or because one sock is sitting lower than the other, or because his smile is too white, you could very well miss out on something huge. You have *got* to start giving people a fair chance to make you happy, Holly. It's time for you to let yourself live."

"Don't you think you're being a little bit dramatic?" I really hate it when people are right.

"When was the last time you got some dick, Holly?"

"Personal, much?" I asked, avoiding the topic.

"It was a week after you had graduated from college. From a guy named Herman. Now, I don't know if Herman was a pity fuck because his parents hated him, or if he was just hung like an ox, but that was almost half a decade ago, girl. Your kitty is hungry for some real meat. I'm not saying run out and marry the dude, but for the love of all things Cher, let him pop the cork on your vacuum sealed vagina before the damn thing grows over and vanishes completely."

"You're disgusting," I chastised, trying not to smile, "and his name wasn't Herman. It was Herbert."

"His name doesn't matter," he rose and headed for the door, "I'm still right and you know it."

"My vagina is fine!" I yelled as he stepped into the hallway.

"Use it or lose it, honey!" he yelled back as he made his way back to his desk.

Killing him had suddenly become a very viable option.

I scrolled through my mental contact list for someone that would have my side and tell me that I'm right. I had to know *someone* who would advise me not to sleep with the richest porn star on the planet.

Somehow, I came up empty handed.

Moments like that made me wish that I could just pick up the phone and call my mother. She would've been the voice of reason. She would have known all the right things to say, asked all the right questions, and, in the long run, convinced me that it had been *my* idea to sleep with him all along.

"I'm so screwed," I complained to my pen holder.

I put my head down on my desk and tried to block out all thoughts of Porter Hale and the traitors that I called best friends. I couldn't find a *good* reason not to pursue something with Porter.

David Michael

There were lots of *bad* reasons and shallow excuses, but nothing that could convince me to forget the way my body lit up every time he looked at me.

I could tell myself that I wasn't attracted to him until I was blue in the face: My body would still call bullshit.

I pushed myself back against my chair, squared my shoulders, and took several deep, calming breaths.

"Okay," I encouraged myself, "I'm gonna say it out loud. Acceptance is the first step to recovery, right?" I sounded like an idiot, even to myself, but I needed a pep talk in a bad way before I allowed the next words out of my mouth.

"I like him. A lot."

The knots in my stomach gave way to butterflies and I could feel the smile tugging at the corners of my mouth. I was practically giddy.

"Like who?"

My eyes snapped open and I jumped, tipping my chair dangerously far back. My arms pin wheeled out to the sides and my legs shot forward to try and regain my balance.

All of my attempts were in vain. I could feel the chair going over and I was powerless to stop it. The world moved in slow motion as Preston's shocked face disappeared from my sight and I found myself staring at the ceiling. My legs were still sticking straight up in the air and my skirt was slowly sliding up my thighs.

I lay there frozen for several seconds, deeply considering the merits of faking a head injury or coma. I finally blew out the breath I'd been holding since the fall and let my legs relax over the edge of the chair.

Preston's worried face appeared between the ceiling and me.

"You okay?" he quickly extended a hand to help me up.

"I'm fine," I groaned as I accepted his hand.

"Are you always this graceful?" he asked once I was on my feet.

"Usually," I ran a hand over my hair, embarrassed.

He hefted my chair upright and made a show of brushing it off.

94

"No harm no foul!" He had the most disarming smile I'd ever seen, "It's as good as new!"

"What the hell are you doing here?" The question shot out of my mouth as more an accusation than anything and I fumbled to smooth it over, "I mean, I didn't know you were dropping by. There's nothing on my schedule. Mitch usually announces when someone's here to see me. I was surprised is all."

Stop talking now, Holly.

"Mitch," he smiled, "He's cute. He told me I'd need an appointment to see you. Put up a fuss about you not accepting walk-ins. He's pretty good at his job, Holly. Fortunately for me, I'm Roman Ruff. All I had to do was take off my shades and flash him a smile. He turned into an adorable little puppy dog and happily pointed me in the direction of your office."

So Mitch was a Hale family fanboy. That explained a lot.

"So you broke my assistant and scared the shit out of me all in one visit? I commend your ability to make an entrance, but that still doesn't answer my question." I returned to my chair and motioned for him to sit in the chair Mitch had recently vacated mere minutes before. "What can I do for you, Preston, my dear?"

He sat down and slid a manila envelope across my desk, "I just wanted to drop this off and say hi."

I eyed him suspiciously, "You drove to my office, wooed my secretary, and gave me a heart attack for the sake of saying hello?"

"Yep!" There was that smile again.

He glanced down at his watch and clapped his hands together before announcing, "I think I've done enough damage around here for the day! I better get out of here before I start a riot."

He rose to leave and I hurried to walk him out.

He turned before I could catch up to him and, with one hand on the door, said, "You really did a number on my brother at dinner last weekend. Keep it up. His ego could use a little abuse."

I stopped in my tracks and stood there with my mouth hanging open and eyes wide.

"See you around, Holly!" and he was gone.

David Michael

My brain was having a hard time translating what I'd just heard. There were a billion and a half questions buzzing around in my head and I damn near ran out the door to chase him through the parking lot. Had Porter talked to him about me? What had he said? Did he think I was an awful bitch for the way I had run out on dinner? Why the hell did Preston think I had done a number on his brother? I beat up Porter's ego?

Mitch burst into the room a few seconds later, pulling me out of my stunned reverie.

"Oh my god, Holly! Ohmygod ohmygod ohmygod! I can't believe Roman Ruff was just here! Why the hell didn't you tell me he was so much sexier in person? I almost swooned, Holly! *Me!* I don't swoon!"

In all the years that I had known and worked with Mitchel Michaelson, I had *never* seen him act like this. There were A-list actors in and out of the office all day every day and not once had he ever been outwardly star-struck by anyone.

I couldn't stop the giggle that bubbled out of me.

"Holly Nash, this is no laughing matter! What the hell is wrong with me?"

I sat down in one of the chairs in front of my desk and he sat in the one next to me.

"You were just in here telling me to bang Porter and completely ignored the fact that my vagina started a revolt the moment I saw him. Now you're in here complaining to me because you got dickmatized by Preston. If this isn't a laughing matter, Mitch, I don't know what is!"

I broke into another fit of giggles when his only response was to furrow his brow at me and pout.

"I'm beginning to think the entire family made a pact with the devil to give them power over all sex organs." The look on his face as he spoke was priceless.

My fit of laughter was renewed as I remembered my conversation with Becks.

"You need to call Becks and tell her that," I wiped the tears of laughter from my cheeks, "She doesn't believe me."

"Ooooh!" he jumped to his feet, "She'll be *way* more excited about this than you are!"

He ran out of my office without even waving goodbye.

I shook my head and smiled as the last of my giggles subsided. At least someone else could suddenly understand my pain.

The envelope Preston had left on my desk caught my eye and curiosity finally got the best of me. I leaned forward and scooped it up, turning the blank yellow paper over in my hands looking for some kind of hint as to what to expect when I opened it.

I slid my finger under the flap and carefully pulled it open. The glue easily gave way and I reached inside to retrieve the contents.

Three pieces of paper had never felt so heavy.

Porter's brilliant blue eyes stared up at me from the first page. It was a headshot printed on thick, glossy card stock. I could tell he'd gone through the entire gamut of professional styling for the shoot and he looked *almost* as good as he did in person. His smile was warm and welcoming and the leather jacket he wore gave him just the right touch of bad boy to spark the tingle deep inside of me. I quickly put the photo face down on my desk before things got out of hand.

The next page appeared to be a résumé. There were a *lot* of blatantly adult films, a few that could go either way, and a brief but impressive stint in musical theatre.

The last page raised more questions than my conversation with Preston had.

It was a white piece of cheap printer paper that you would find on most fax machines all over the world. Four words handwritten across the center in bold black marker had my head spinning with uncertainty.

Give him a chance.

Thirteen
Porter

I sat on my couch and sipped at a beer while I waited for Parker to arrive.

He had sent me a text message that morning asking if he could come over and talk. He even offered to bring food.

Something was wrong. I could feel it in my gut.

He hadn't asked to come over and talk in years. We had all just gotten so busy that slowing down and just hanging out together wasn't an option for us anymore. Given his situation and the fact that I hadn't heard from him since the fight at Preston's house, I cancelled the plans I had already made and bought a case of beer.

Three rapid knocks followed by two slow knocks signaled my brother's arrival. It had been his signature knock since we were kids.

The door opened a moment later and Parker walked into my condo with his arms full of takeout containers.

I slid the remotes to one side of the coffee table and set the books I kept there on the end table next to me.

He set the boxes down and sat on the couch with a groan, "I hate the traffic in this city. Can we move somewhere else and choose a new mecca for the porn industry, please? Somewhere out of the way, preferably. Boise maybe?"

"Too bum-fuck for me. Preston might go for it, actually," I smiled over at him, "I hear there are a lot of Mormons there though. I don't think they're overly-excited about the adult film industry."

"Mmm," he nodded and reached for the nearest box, "Good point."

Porter

Something was different about him. He was focused, his eyes were clear, he wasn't twitchy, and I hadn't seen him brush at his nose once since he'd walked in.

"Parker," I couldn't stop the smile that spread across my face, "Are you sober?"

He smiled into his food without making eye contact again, "Yeah."

"Bro! That's huge! How long? You're looking great!"

"Since that morning at Preston's. I called Mom that day and kinda spilled my guts. She actually went with me to my first N.A. meeting the next day. I stayed at her house for the first week while I detoxed. It wasn't pretty, Porter," he still hadn't looked up from his Chinese, "but she took care of me. I was a real asshole. I'd get restless and then get pissed off about being stuck in the house, which would just make me more restless. I felt like a caged animal. I tried to leave a few times even when she begged me to stay. I made it as far as the main gate once. Did you know that she owns a beanbag cannon? I woke up in cold sweats every night from the nightmares, but she never left my bedside. She was there with water and an ear every time. I must've kept her awake for three days straight. It's a wonder she didn't kill me. Then I wanted to do nothing but eat and sleep. I probably owe her thousands of dollars for all the Pop Tarts I ate. Anyway, fourteen days clean and sober."

I was at a loss for words. Very few things had the ability to shock me into silence, but that conversation wasn't one I had ever expected to have.

He finally looked over at me and what I saw in his eyes gutted me.

There was nothing but pain staring back at me. It was like talking about it forced him to live the entire experience all over again. There was a familiar light that I had grown accustomed to seeing in them and I wanted it back. At that moment, I would have given anything to see my little brother smile again.

Say something, you idiot!

"I've been a real asshole for the last couple of years, Porter. I'll make it up to you somehow. I promise."

99

"Parker, you don't owe me anything. This is the best thing you could ever give me. Stay sober. That's all I need from you."

A shadow of the smile I was looking for curved his lips.

"You remember how I ate everything in Mom's house? That part hasn't gone away yet. I'm starving to death. Let's eat?"

"Sure," I stood to grab plates, but he grabbed my arm before my ass had completely left the couch.

"Porter, we don't have cooties. We can eat out of the boxes."

I smiled at the memory of sharing takeout from the box with Parker and Preston as teenagers, "Of course. Want a beer?"

"No," his right leg started bouncing, "That's been the hardest part. Drinking just makes me want a line and I think the point of sobriety is to avoid wanting a line."

"I'm such an asshole! Do you want something else? I've got water, milk, juice, and quite possibly a random case of Capri Suns. Which I may or may not have bought for myself this morning."

The glimmer returned to his eyes and a huge smile split his face as he let loose with unbridled laughter, "Capri Sun sounds great. Thanks."

I grabbed a bottle of beer and a pouch of juice from the half-empty box. I caught the door to the fridge just before it closed and glanced down at the beer in my hand.

Such a douche.

I returned the beer to the shelf in the door and grabbed a shiny silver packet of sugar water for myself.

"Heads up!" I tossed the childhood favorite into his waiting hands.

"Thanks. For everything."

I knew what he was saying, but couldn't think of anything appropriate to say in response. I nodded at him and flashed him a smile as I jabbed my plastic straw through the foil pouch in my hand. I lifted it toward him in salute, "Cheers to you, to life, and to mom."

He touched his juice to mine and we each took a sip.

"Let's eat."

I expressed my agreement by ripping open a box of fried rice and practically dumping it down my throat.

"It's a good thing I got two orders of that!"

I swallowed, mostly without chewing, "You know fried rice is my favorite."

He laughed and opened his own box of the salty fried-rice goodness, "I do. And orange chicken, broccoli beef, and for good measure, a double order of crab wantons."

"Have I ever told you that you're my favorite brother?"

"Only every time I buy you Chinese food."

"Good. Because it's true."

"Until Preston buys you Chinese food."

"Well, you can't *always* be the favorite! There's enough of me to go around!"

We ate the rest of our meal in silence. There was barely enough time to breathe, let alone speak. Parker took a break from inhaling dinner just long enough to replenish our Capri Suns. He immediately returned to his gigantic helping of orange chicken.

When the last grain of rice had been chased out of the last container we both leaned back against the couch and sighed, content.

"I'm a little bit sad every time I eat Chinese food. I know I'll just be hungry again in twenty minutes. But holy shit that was delicious." I sucked up the last of my juice and tossed the pouch on top of the pile of empty cardboard containers.

Parker's head rested against the back of the couch and he was staring absently at the ceiling, worrying his bottom lip.

"That was a poop joke, Parker. You didn't laugh. What's on your mind?"

"I talked to Preston today. He's still pissed and not nearly as optimistic as you are. It was a little rough is all. I'm still trying to figure out how I'm gonna make things right with him."

"Shit." Preston was notorious for holding wicked grudges. "I'm pretty sure he's still pissed at me for the time I let him take the fall for my bong. He didn't talk to me for a month after that."

"This is a little bit bigger than us leaving your bong in his room, Porter."

"I know that, Parker. I was trying to empathize. How do you want me to handle this? Do you want me to tell you that the best thing you can do is leave him be until he gets over it? Is that the truth you want to hear? Sadly, it'll be torture on you the entire time. If you want to make amends, you have to wait until he's receptive. If you try to go at him for forgiveness right now, he'll throw it in your face and spew whatever venom he has toward you without feeling bad for it. If you wanna stay on the wagon, I don't recommend putting yourself through that."

"I know. I only got the tip of the iceberg today. I've fucked up in some big ways over the years and I didn't expect him to just forgive and forget over night. Hell, I didn't expect *you* to be so cool about it. You've spent *years* beating yourself up over my mistakes and I let you do it. No more, Porter. You hear me? If I fuck up again, it's *my* mistake, not yours. I'm an adult, capable of making my own choices and dealing with the consequences."

Who the hell was this guy and where had he come from? Since he was old enough to talk, Parker had *always* been one to point the finger at everyone but himself. Accepting that his actions affected other people wasn't something I'd ever seen him do.

"After he finished telling me how it was only a matter of time before I slipped up, he *did* give me an interesting bit of information about *you* though," he smiled again, one of the toothy, genuine smiles our family was known for.

"Oh, God. That worries me."

"I'm told you have a lady friend! That bombshell from the premier party? What was her name?"

"Holly," I muttered as I got up to get a beer, "and I wouldn't call her a friend."

"Holly. That's right. Holly Nash, the casting director. Preston says she really did a number on you. Got you all tied up in knots over what she thinks and shit."

"She's a meal ticket, Park. Nothing more. I care what she thinks about me because she is one of the biggest names in her industry and I want to get the hell out of porn."

"Does she know she's just a meal ticket? Have you told her this?"

"Of course not!" I yelled from the fridge, "You know how it is. You've gotta play the game if you wanna get a foot up anywhere.

Especially coming from the porn industry. I'm a PR *nightmare.* It's going to be hell to get anyone to take me on and give me any kind of serious role because half the planet has seen me with my dick buried in some floozie."

"Preston said he went and saw her today."

I set my beer down on the counter and stepped around the half wall that separated the kitchen from the living room.

"What?"

"Yeah. He had just gotten home from her office when I called him. Wouldn't give me any details, but he was there with your lady friend."

"Hmm," I mused, "I knew they were friends before the party, but I didn't think they were the kind of friends that dropped in on each other at work."

I left my beer sitting on the counter and rejoined him on the couch.

"You should tell her what you're after, Porter. What's the worst that can happen? If you don't care about this woman, she can say no and you can move on to trying to catch your break like the rest of this state."

"You know I don't handle rejection well. I've done everything I can to ensure that nobody says no to me. I spend fourteen hours a week at the gym, I get my teeth whitened once a month, I play it safe when it comes to close relationships, and I always surround myself with people who I *know* support me in anything I want to do. Nobody has the power to make or break my career that way except me."

"Don't you think we're a little old to be playing it safe, Porter?"

When did my little brothers become fonts of wisdom?

"Honestly?" I sighed, "I don't know. And that's what scares me. Since Dad died, I feel like I've just fucked up at every turn. As the man of the house, I should've made sure you guys stayed in school. I was making *plenty* of money to make sure you guys were taken care of long enough to graduate. I shouldn't have let you get pulled into this shit. If we hadn't have followed in his footsteps, you probably wouldn't be—"

"I told you no-fucking-more of that shit, Porter. The choices I made and the life I lead are *my* problems. Not yours. They always have been. You made the choice to follow Dad down this path, and so did we. You didn't force us into anything. Whatever has or hasn't happened as a result of our choices is on our shoulders, not yours." He had pushed himself off the couch and was pacing back and forth across my living room.

"I still should've been a better role model for you guys."

"No, Porter, if *anyone* should've been a better role model, it's Dad. But it's in the past and not something we can change. It's something we can live with and move the fuck on. If you want something more for yourself, now's the time to go after it. You're not responsible for Preston and me anymore. We're both a little bit fucked up, but we're big boys. We can handle it. You're not as perfect as you'd like the world to believe either. Tell her, Porter. Make her see that you're worth the risk."

I knew arguing with him wouldn't get me anywhere, so I let my head fall back against the couch and tried my best not to grumble under my breath.

"I don't even know where to start, Park."

"I can't help you there," he ran a hand through his dirty blond hair and dropped onto the couch next to me, "I *can* tell you that lying to women is a *bad* idea. She'll sniff out your bullshit. If you piss her off, she'll find your weakness, and she'll stick her well-manicured finger in it. Be honest with her and get it over with. You're the biggest porn star on the planet at the moment. What the hell do you have to be worried about?"

"Thanks, Park." I clapped a hand on his back, "I'll think about it. This shit is a mess. You got some time for some mindless xBox?"

"Actually," he glanced down at his watch, "I've gotta be to a meeting across town in twenty. I've gotta bounce."

He stood up and I rose to walk him out.

Parker pulled me into a hug and slapped my back. I was stunned. It felt like someone had pulled all the muscles out of my arms and I couldn't move. He hadn't shown me that kind of affection since we were kids.

Porter

I finally convinced one of my hands to pat his back in a halfhearted hug and he let me go with a smile.

Before he closed the door behind him, he winked at me and said, "Tell her you like her, Porter. Everyone knows except the two of you. Take the risk. Give yourself the chance to be happy. You've earned it."

The door closed and left me standing in the middle of my living room wondering what the fuck was happening to my life. *Both* of my younger brothers had called me out and given me life advice. *Good* life advice at that.

Preston and I needed to have a talk.

I fished my cell out of the couch cushions where it had fallen and booted up the screen.

I froze when I saw that I had a single text message. From Holly Nash.

"Could this day *possibly* get any more fucking weird?"

I swiped the screen and read the message. My palms instantly started to sweat.

We need to talk. Noon tomorrow. 101 Coffee on Franklin.

Fourteen
Holly

"It's just business, Holly. Calm down."

I had been repeating those words to myself since the moment my feet hit the floor that morning. I was practically vibrating with excitement. If this meeting with Porter went well, I'd not only have a new client, but I'd have the chance to work with him more often so I could secretly feed the demands of my infatuation.

"Holly?" Mitch poked his head into my office as I was gathering up my purse.

"What's up?" I asked as I dropped my cell inside the miniature tote bag.

"Oh! Are you taking off already?"

"Yeah. I've got a meeting at noon. I'll probably be out of the office the rest of the day, but you can call me if you need anything."

"I didn't see anything on your schedule for today." He was suspicious.

"This one's being kept on the down low. If it goes well, the agency stands to make a lot of money. I just don't want any potential problems to arise before I've had a chance to really feel it out myself."

I regretted the words as soon as they left my mouth. The idea of feeling Porter for *any* reason shot straight through me like a red-hot poker. I didn't need to get any more myself worked up before I even saw him. That would end in disaster for my poor sex drive. Hell, I'd probably just burst into flames.

"Alright," he stepped to the side as I walked into the hall, "let me know how your date with Porter goes then!"

I spun to face him, "How did you know?"

He flashed me a wicked grin, "I didn't."

"Ugh," I rolled my eyes and continued to the front doors, "You're such an ass. Don't say anything to anyone. Preston dropped off a cryptic package when he was in here yesterday and I just want to get a feel for how serious this is before I say anything official."

"Mum's the word, love," he returned to his chair behind his desk and propped his chin on his palms like a little cherub, "But if you end up sleeping with him and don't tell me, I *will* quit. I'm serious this time, Holly."

I waved a dismissive hand at him in acknowledgment and pushed my way through the double doors and into the parking lot.

Lunch hour traffic was bound to be a bitch and I chastised myself for not leaving a little bit earlier. I'd look like a total bitch if he beat me there.

I nosed out into the street and gunned it, narrowly avoiding a few bumpers and completely ignoring the blaring horns.

I cranked up the volume on my stereo and did my best to sing along with the top forty pop that blared out of the speakers.

It was a clear, sunny day, not all that unusual for southern California, and I crawled along with the rest of traffic with my windows down. I didn't have a lot of time to spend on the beach working on my tan, so every chance I got to hang an arm out the window while I drove was one I couldn't pass up.

By the time I pulled into the tiny lot behind the coffee shop, I was five minutes late. I glanced around for Porter's Land Rover and did an internal happy dance when I didn't see the monstrosity among the cars in the lot.

My small celebration ended abruptly as I stepped out of the sweltering heat into the cool air-conditioned building. Porter was seated at the counter on one of the art-deco stools.

He glanced over his shoulder at the sound of the bell over the door and his eyes lit up when he saw me.

At least, that's what I told myself.

"Sorry I'm late," I apologized as I set my purse on the counter next to him, "I hate traffic in this city."

"No worries," he assured me, "I was almost late myself. I had to drive like a maniac to get here on time."

"You drove? I didn't see the Rover in the lot out back. Is there some secret underground parking garage I don't know about?"

He laughed and I had to fight the urge to faint as a giddy thrill raced through my body at the sound. His brilliant blue eyes sparkled when he laughed.

"No. I left the Rover at home today. I wanted to get out on the bike while the weather was so nice."

That explained the leather jacket.

"You ride?"

He nodded his head and spun around on his stool to point through one of the windows.

"Holy shit, Porter." I couldn't pull my eyes away from the most beautiful piece of machinery I had ever seen.

"She's pretty, isn't she?" He said the words like he was talking about a child.

"Is that a Panhead? Forty-eight, I think." I rushed over to the window and pressed my face against the glass like a kid in a candy store.

"Holly Nash, you are full of surprises."

His voice was dangerously close. I could feel his breath on my ear and it sent a shudder down my spine.

I took a wide step to the side and reluctantly tore my eyes away from the classic Harley to face him.

"My mom had a thing for bikers after my dad died. I've seen a lot of pretty bikes in my life, but I've only ever seen one other bike like this in my life. It had been ridden well though. Yours is pristine!"

He smiled again, sending another jolt of need through my body.

"I've had a lot of work done on her. She's my baby."

"I'd say..."

The frame and body were in mint condition. The massive whitewall tires complimented the powder blue paint and white pin stripes to perfection. The massive leather seat sat on top of two brand new springs and the chrome pipes glinted brightly in the sunlight.

"You've gotta let me ride it," I begged.

"Woah now!" he took a few steps backwards and held up his hands, "Don't get crazy on me! *Nobody* rides my bike. Nobody even *sits* on my bike. That's part of the reason I bought it! There's no way to put a bitch seat on the back of that thing, so I don't have to let anyone else near her."

"Porter," I leveled my gaze on him, "I grew up on motorcycles. That bike is not just any bike. It's a fucking *legend*. You can't tell me no. Please don't tell me no."

"I'm telling you no." The expression on his face told me it was the end of the conversation—for the time being.

I promised myself then and there that I would ride that bike someday.

"Fine," I said, casting one last longing glance through the window, "Let's get down to business then."

We returned to our seats at the counter and placed our drink orders with the barista.

"Your brother came to see me at work yesterday," I said casually.

"So I've heard."

"So he told you about our little visit then?" My heart rate spiked at the possibility that Preston had spilled the beans about my crush.

"Not exactly," he folded his arms over his chest causing his biceps to strain against the cotton of his tee shirt, "He told Parker that he was at your office and Parker told me."

Oh thank God.

"Well," I tried for my best business voice, "Your resume is impressive. You know as well as I do that your current line of employment leaves a lot to be desired as far as PR goes, but I think if you can land a few good roles and keep your nose clean for a couple years, we could build you a pretty solid career in mainstream film. Now, I want to focus mostly on your musical theatre days," I fished the manila envelope out of my purse and retrieved his résumé, "There are some pretty major roles on this list, Porter. I was more than a little impressed, to be honest. Do you know of any critical reviews that you could dig up for me?"

I glanced over at him at that point and was surprised to see his mouth hanging open. He was staring at the piece of paper in my hand like it might catch on fire and explode at any moment.

It dawned on me that he had no idea why Preston had been in my office.

"You didn't know he was dropping this off?"

He slowly shook his head from side to side, still not saying anything.

"I see," I returned the sheet of paper to the envelope and held it out to him, "I apologize for the confusion. I assumed you had asked him to drop it off on your behalf. It's impossible to get into our agency without a solid referral from an agent or someone with a foot in the door. I thought I understood that you wanted to be one of our clients."

Something I said seemed to snap him out of his stupor.

"Absolutely!" he cranked up the charm with another dazzling smile, "I just... I had no idea that this is what was coming! I thought this was your way of paying me back for our botched dinner date! I wasn't expecting a business meeting!"

I lowered the envelope into my lap, "So you *are* interested?"

"Hell yes I'm interested!" He drummed his hands on the counter and *barely* managed to contain the excitement I could see buzzing through him.

I couldn't help but chuckle.

"Good," I smiled as the barista set our coffees on the counter, "I'll get the ball rolling then. You'll have to come in and meet with the rest of the casting directors and of course we'll have to get approval to take you on as a client, but I don't see it being *too* much of an issue. There are bound to be some bumps, but nothing I can't handle."

I held up my coffee in toast, "To new business ventures."

He touched his own cup to mine and we sipped.

He practically threw his cup down on the counter in his excitement and jumped out of his chair. He leaned over and placed his hands on my knees, spreading warmth up my thighs, "Holly, we *have* to go celebrate! You have no idea how much this means to me!"

His excitement was infectious. I could feel it bubbling up in my own chest and I couldn't wipe the smile off my face.

"Say you'll come spend the day with me! Please!"

He was almost bouncing up and down and it was the most adorable thing I'd ever seen.

"Okay, okay!" I laughed, placing my hands on his shoulders to keep him from shaking me, "What did you have in mind?"

"It's a surprise!" He hummed, almost squealed, with excitement, "I'll just need you to follow me to my condo so I can drop the bike off. Then we can either take your car or switch it out for the Land Rover. We'll decide there! Holy shit, Holly! I can't believe this just happened!"

He plopped back down on the stool next to me and spun it around in circles.

I'm surprised he didn't hoot and holler like a mad man.

"You should probably call Preston at some point," I grinned, "You owe him."

"Trust me," he planted his feet on the ground and stopped the stool from spinning, "I will."

We finished up our drinks and he gave me his address, just in case I lost him on the bike, and we headed out.

It took a whole three minutes before he darted between two cars and took off like a shot.

I pulled up at the address he gave me and shook my head.

"You've gotta be kidding me," I muttered to the steering wheel.

My phone started ringing from its cradle on the dashboard. I hit the green telephone button on my steering wheel and answered with, "Really, Porter? The Ritz-Carlton? Don't you think that's a little over the top?"

The sound of his laughter came through my speakers and filled my car. Porter Hale in stereo was a whole new level of torture for my hormones.

"When you can have anything you want," I could hear the smile in his voice, "why settle for less than the best?"

The line went dead and a split second later, there was a knock on my window. A shrill squeak jumped out of my throat and I turned my head to face the offending knuckles.

I rolled down the window and let loose barrages of swear words that would've made my father proud.

Porter just laughed at me and shook his head. "A pretty lady like you shouldn't know words like that," he said when I had finished, "Are we taking your car?"

"Get your ass in here, you idiot."

He jogged around the front of my car, running an appreciative finger over the hood, and let himself in the passenger side.

"Where, are we going, Miss Daisy?"

He made a show of primping an imaginary bob cut and clutched a string of invisible pearls at his throat. "Well," the thick southern drawl he used was surprisingly accurate and forced a laugh out of me, "I do believe there are some *lovely* tide pools down at Dana Point if that's the kind of thing that interests you. There's a Wayland Gallery in Laguna that carries some *amazing* pieces, and, if you're feeling particularly adventurous, there's also a paddle board rental shop on the beach next door."

I could see the challenge in his eyes as he spoke the last sentence and something inside of me rose to the occasion. There was no way in hell I'd let him win this game.

I put the car in drive and pulled away from the curb, slamming on the gas and darting into traffic like a crazy person. I watched him in my peripheral, hoping to see him flinch or grab for the "oh shit" handle above his door.

The bastard didn't move a single muscle. He remained completely relaxed and his giant goofy smile never faltered once.

I maneuvered through the city traffic and onto the freeway like a precision driver and let the horses beneath the hood carry us away.

The great thing about traffic in Los Angeles is the fact that there can be a million cars on the road and, unless some idiot causes an accident, you never come to a stop. Bumper-to-bumper traffic in California just means that everyone drives *really* close together at freeway speeds. Everywhere else I'd ever driven, nobody rushes *anywhere* during rush hour. It's just gridlock for as far as the eye can see.

"What made you pick Audi?" Porter asked as he poked at the buttons on my stereo.

"They're the best," I said simply and swatted at his hand, "I could've spent more money and gone for something a with a little more luxury, but at the price point I paid for this thing, there isn't a better car on the road."

He laughed and went back to messing around with the buttons, "I'll accept that answer. It seems we have more in common than we initially thought."

I quirked an eyebrow and glanced over at him, "What do you mean?"

"Well, we both own what we consider to be the best, we both drive like maniacs, we both know Preston, we both work in the film industry," his smile grew even bigger, "and we both think I'm gorgeous."

"Ha!" I almost swerved into the next lane as I laughed, "Conceited much? Someone needs to poke a hole in that ego of yours before it explodes."

"Are you denying that you want to climb me like a tree?"

No.

"You bet your ass I am!" I lied, "I'm not going to sleep with you, Porter. Two of my best friends have been trying to talk me into it since before I even met you. If *they* can't do it, neither can you. And now you're a client. Conflict of interest much?"

"Hmm..." he hummed thoughtfully, "I see."

I *really* didn't like the sound of that.

I already knew Porter Hale well enough to know he'd *never* give in that easily. He was up to something. Whatever it was, it couldn't possibly be good for me.

"Save us both the trouble and put it out of your head. Give it up. I don't want to have to bury a body this week."

The laugh that burst out of him was sudden and loud, causing me to jump and jerk the wheel to the left. The car went

113

with it, jolting perilously close to the car next to us before I could guide it back into my lane.

"What the hell is wrong with you?" I asked accusingly, "Are you *trying* to get us killed? You almost gave me a damn heart attack!"

"I'm sorry," he said between breaths, "but that was the funniest thing I've heard all day!"

"I don't remember telling any jokes," I glared at him with one eye, keeping the other on the bumper of the car in front of us, "You must be *really* easily amused."

"There were two jokes in there, Holly. The first one being that you think you could do enough damage to have a reason to bury me," he chuckled to himself quietly. "The second being that you think I could put you out of my mind for even a second."

I think my ovaries blushed.

I could feel the heat travelling through my stomach and radiating out into my body like a miniature sun had taken up residence inside my vagina. It was a sensation I had almost grown accustomed to since Porter Hale had trampled his way into my life.

I fought the urge to press my thighs together and hoped that he wouldn't see the flush I could feel creeping up my neck. I didn't want him to know the kind of effect he had on my body. He would absolutely use that knowledge to his advantage and make it a point to reduce me to a babbling, blushing schoolgirl at every opportunity.

"Porter," I sighed, giving him time to interrupt my protest.

"I'm not saying you have to marry me." I scoffed but he ignored it and continued, "Hell, I'm not even saying I want you to stay the night. The only thing I'm saying is that I haven't been able to stop thinking about you since we met. I need to get you out of my system so we can go on with this business relationship you're so intent on having. I can see it in your eyes, Holly. You want me just as bad as I want you. There's nothing that says we can't burn bright for a night and scratch whatever itch it is that we've both got for each other."

"That's the difference between you and I, Porter," I tried to keep my voice calm and level, "Just because I want something, doesn't mean I *have* to have it. You're the cake to my diet. I might crave whatever you've got to give, but I know damn well that it won't be good for me and I'll just hate myself for it in the morning."

"Are you always this cold, Holly? Or is it just with me?"

"You're the only one who has ignored the No Trespassing signs and forced your way into my bubble in a while. So I guess it's just with you."

I could feel my defenses going up and if he didn't drop it, I was going to start saying things I'd probably regret even more than sleeping with him. He was a nice enough guy and didn't deserve that. I had to find a way to distract him and get him to change the topic of conversation for his own sake.

"I know Preston well enough to understand your relationship with him, but I don't know anything about Parker. Preston doesn't really say anything about him and, from what I gather, you guys aren't very close either."

He let out a huff of air telling me I had struck a nerve.

I could only hope that it was better than the one we had been toying with before.

"We used to be close," he began, "The three of us were pretty much inseparable when we were kids. It wasn't until Preston had been in the business for about a year that we really started growing apart. At first I blamed it on our schedules—we were all so damn busy all the time."

I knew there was more coming, but I didn't want to push it. I let him come to it in his own time. It took him a minute, but he finally continued.

"I think I was just in denial for a while. My relationship with Preston never changed. Sure, we didn't see each other as often as we had before, but we still talked on the phone every day. We could still get together and just drink beer and play video games on the random off-day. But Parker had all but disappeared. When we talked on the phone, it was never for more than a few minutes at a time before he had to go. The few times we hung out together in person, he was always twitchy and seemed like he was ready to bolt for the door. I finally just stopped pressing and let him do his thing. I only saw him for family holidays and big events, like Preston's release party. That went on for almost two years."

He still wasn't finished. I could see that he was trying to decide if the next words out of his mouth were words he wanted to share.

"I'm prying," I figured I'd give him an easy out, "You have every right to tell me it's none of my business, Porter."

He made a sound deep in his throat but didn't actually form any words. He stared straight ahead with his brow furrowed and his eyes focused on something in the distance.

Our drive continued in silence, nothing but the sounds of traffic and the low music drifting out of the speakers broke it.

"It was the day after Preston's release party that it all finally came to a head." His words were sudden and surprisingly loud in the quiet space. "Parker's coke problem had gotten out of hand long before then, but we had all just learned to deal with it. Our dad had done the same thing and it never really caused any major problems, we all just stayed out of his way and everything was fine. I realize now that I had always known what was going on with him. I just didn't know what to do to fix it. With our dad being gone, the responsibility of making sure the family remained copacetic fell on my shoulders. When my little brother started getting coked out of his head on a regular basis, it just made me feel like a complete failure. I started to blame myself for not being a better role model. I could see him spinning out of control, but the only thing I could do was stand by and watch. It was like being in a nightmare where an axe-wielding maniac is chasing you, but all you can do is walk. You can't scream for help, you can't run, you can't even close your eyes against what's coming. When everything blew up at Preston's party, I knew we had hit rock bottom."

He looked over at me with hard, gleaming eyes and a clenched jaw.

"Porter," I put my hand over his on the console, doing my best to ignore the sizzling heat that rushed through me when our skin touched, "You can't blame yourself for that. He's an adult. He's going to make his own decisions whether you think they're right or not."

He blew out a breath and made a conscious effort to relax his jaw.

"I know that," he spat. He drew another breath and the next words were much softer, "Everyone, including Parker, has been telling me that lately. It's not the fact that he chose that path that bothers me, Holly. It's the fact that I watched him do it and didn't even *try* to stop him. I buried my head in the sand and turned a blind eye on my little brother."

Just before the 405 merged with Interstate 5, I took the exit onto Highway 133. It would take us through the mountains and drop us right into the center of Laguna Beach. We could decide what we were going to do from there since it was only a ten minute drive to Dana Point.

As the city gave way to the softer, lush landscape of the San Joaquin Hills, Porter finally began to relax again. I turned up the music a few notches and focused on enjoying the ride. The canyon was beautiful, the sky was clear, and I was in my most prized possession with one of the sexiest men on the planet. It was definitely a moment worth savoring.

As we dropped out of the canyon it felt like the whole world opened up before us. The deep blue of the Pacific stretched to the horizon where it met with the cloudless azure sky. The sun was high overhead and the golden sandy beaches stretched north and south for miles.

By the time we hit the Pacific Coast Highway, I was itching for a day in the sun and Porter was spouting off random information about the city.

"Look!" he pointed out his window at statue of a homeless-looking guy, "That's The Waver! I remember coming here when I was a kid and it never failed, *every* day, rain or shine, he was out standing on that corner waving and smiling at the passers-by. He died a while back and it was kind of like a piece of my childhood went with him. I was happy to see them put that statue up."

"He just stood there and waved all day?"

"Yep," Porter smiled over at me, his entire face radiating his happiness, "Wouldn't that be the life? Nothing to do, no obligations, your only appointment every day being to stand on the corner and make someone else's world a little bit brighter?"

I thought about his words for a moment, "I don't think I could do it. I mean, in theory it's a wonderful idea, but think of the hardships that would come along with it. Never knowing where your next meal would come from, unsure of where you'd be sleeping at night—what would you do if you got sick? I doubt he had health insurance."

Porter's smile never faltered, "You worry too much, Holly Nash. Park right here!"

I pulled into the stall he pointed to and we got out of the car.

The crisp smell of a coastal southern California summer hit me like a physical force. Massive gardens filled with Birds of Paradise bloomed throughout the grassy strip between the street and the sand. The wonderfully sweet scent mixed perfectly with the gentle brine of ocean air and I drew a deep breath through my nose. I closed my eyes and let it wash over me for a moment while I enjoyed the warmth of the sun beating down on me.

I opened them just in time to see Porter's back disappear into a board shop a few doors down.

I locked the car and darted after him, not wanting to get left behind and miss the adventures.

"Thirty-two C?" he asked as I entered the shop behind him. He held up a white and red bikini and raised an eyebrow. "This would look good on you."

If I were honest with myself, it's probably the one I would have picked, too.

"No way," I moved to the rack and flicked through the bathing suits until I found the one that would've been my second choice, "I like this one better."

"At least I was right about your cup size." He snatched the bikini out of my hand and headed deeper into the store. I rolled my eyes and followed him.

He was rifling through the board shorts and quickly grabbed a black pair with hot pink pin stripes, "This'll do."

"I like this one more," I pouted as I reached for the rack.

Porter

When I held up the tiny pair of grape smugglers he laughed out loud. A nearby employee gave us the stink eye before she went back to folding tee shirts.

"Fine," he took the swimsuit from me, returned the board shorts, and headed to the counter without another word.

"Porter!" I laughed, "I was just kidding! The board shorts are fine!"

"No way!" he countered, "These are the ones you picked. I'm a people pleaser, Holly. You'll learn this about me. This little Japanese sling shot makes you happy, so it's what you're stuck with."

He dropped the two suits on the counter and distractedly pulled two pair of flip-flops off the rack next to the register.

"Oh!" he snapped his fingers, "Can't forget sunglasses!"

He chose two pair at random from a nearby stand and added them to the pile.

"Is this everything for you today?" the teenager behind the counter asked.

"We'll need some SPF 15 as well, please," he turned to me, "Skin care is more important than people think."

I just smiled and shook my head. I already knew that Porter Hale was a force to be reckoned with when he set his mind to something. Nothing I could say would get him to change his mind or let me at least pay for my own bathing suit.

While he was paying for his pile of treasures, I slipped away to one of the far walls and gathered up a few of my own.

He was just taking the receipt from the cashier when I returned and dumped my armful of stuff on the counter, "Go change," I commanded as he stood there smiling at me like a kid in a candy store.

"You're buying us sandcastle toys and boogie boards? Holly Nash, you surprise me." He sauntered off toward the dressing rooms and I returned my attention to the task at hand.

"Is this everything for you today?" the girl repeated robotically.

"That should be it," I confirmed with a smile.

"Your total comes to forty-five twenty-seven."

I handed her my AmEx.

"You were right," Porter's voice behind me made me jump, "I like this one better."

I turned to face him and my eyes must've bugged out of my head because he bent in half laughing at me. When he came up for air, his eyes were watering and his face was red.

"Oh my God, Holly!" he said through gasps of breath, "I wish you could see your face right now!"

I knew my mouth was hanging open, but I couldn't do anything to stop it. My eyes were glued to the tiny strip of cloth slung across his hips. If the thing were any smaller his balls would've popped out of either side. There was *nothing* left to my imagination.

"How do you not have any tan lines?"

That's all you can come up with? Idiot.

The questions must've surprised him, too, because his eyebrows nearly disappeared into his hairline.

"You've got Ryder Ruff in a Speedo standing in front of you and all you can think about is tan lines? You're gonna be a tougher nut to bust than I thought!"

I could feel the flush creeping into my face again as the thought of him busting any kind of nut overtook my imagination and went on a brief, but intense joy ride with my sensibilities.

I knew he had done it on purpose the moment he flashed me that mischievous grin I had come to both adore and loathe.

"You, sir, are an asshole."

I turned back around and quickly scrawled my signature across the receipt on the counter. I shoved my toys into his arms and took the bag of clothes from his hand before stomping off to the dressing room to change.

I opened the bag to retrieve my beachwear and grumbled to myself when his clothes were balled up on top. I dumped the entire contents on the floor and picked up the bikini my stubborn ass had picked.

"Boxer briefs," I noted with a grin as I removed the tags from my top, "I'm surprised he doesn't go commando for easy access."

Porter

I changed quickly and neatly folded my work outfit before placing it in the bag. As I bent to scoop up his clothes, an idea struck me that had a wicked grin spreading across my face.

I fished my phone out of the bag then dumped his socks, jeans, and tee shirt back into it before scooping up his underwear by the waistband. I used the front-facing camera to snap a selfie with the coveted undergarment and fired it off to Becks and Mitch with the caption, "Look what I've got…"

I returned my phone to the bottom of the bag and left the dressing room to rejoin Porter.

"Let's go dump this in the car and hit the sand!"

He had picked up two beach towels while I changed and nodded his agreement, "My sandcastle is gonna kick your sandcastle's ass."

The jab spurred my competitive streak and I shot back, "Game on."

We deposited our clothes and phones in the trunk of my car and headed for the beach.

It was busy, but not crowded, so we didn't have any problems finding a spot out of the way of the volleyball games and sunbathers close to the water. He dumped our toys, towels, and sunblock unceremoniously and took off like a bullet for the water.

The spray of sand kicked up by his bare feet quickly gave way to a spray of water as he splashed through the surf. I couldn't help but laugh as he did the surfer run through the waves, lifting his knees as high as they'd go and kicking his legs out to the side.

He dived headfirst into an oncoming wave and disappeared beneath the surface. I shook my head as I tried to stifle my giggles and turned my attention to the pile at my feet. I'm not a water person, so joining his swim was absolutely out of the question. I shook off the towels and laid them out on top of the hot sand before crawling on top of the pink one and grabbing the sun block.

I had a tan to work on while my porn star date frolicked in the ocean. If he returned with some kind of device for me to float on, I might consider joining him. Until then, it was time to get brown.

Once I was sufficiently slathered, I pressed the cheap sunglasses onto my nose and laid back to enjoy the sun, the surf, and the fact that I wasn't stuck in my office.

I'm not sure how long it took, but I eventually drifted off to sleep.

I dreamt of Porter.

Fifteen
Porter

Ocean swimming had always been one of my favorite workouts. Fighting the currents just gives an extra boost to all those stabilizer muscles that you don't normally work out.

I had probably been in the water for a good twenty minutes by the time I finally dragged myself out of the surf and back onto solid ground. It took me a few moments to reorient myself and remember where I had dumped our stuff.

I'd been carried a few hundred yards south of the surf shop where I'd bought our swimsuits, so I used that as a marker and made my way north. I constantly scanned the bodies on the beach looking for Holly.

I was almost certain that she would've followed me into the water and tried to out-swim me. I had seen the glint of defiance in her eyes each time I posed even a subtle challenge. I'd been a little excited to get the first contest underway.

She was lying on a towel a few dozen yards off when I spotted her. It didn't take me long to realize that she had fallen asleep. I couldn't stop the grin that spread across my face as I thought of all the ways I could mess with her just to get her riled up.

I stood over her, considering my options, and quickly became hypnotized by the gentle rise and fall of her breasts. She was definitely a California girl. She had a flawless beach tan, a body that *screamed* for a bikini, and perfectly smooth legs that could only be attained by a girl who had experience in being beach-ready at all times.

I wanted to reach down and run my hands up them.

A quick shake of the head broke the spell her body had put on me. The droplets of water that fell from my hair onto her body were just enough to gently pull her out of her slumber.

"How long was I out?" she asked groggily.

"I'm not sure. I was out there for about twenty minutes, I think. I thought you'd follow me."

She sat up and stretched, pressing her breasts against the thin cotton of her top, "I'm not big on the idea of being in water I can't see through. Put me in a boat and I'm fine, but I'm not about to swim out there and become shark bait."

My eyes rolled in their sockets. *Jaws* must have ruined her.

"Well, at least you didn't burn. That would've put a damper on things. Roll over and let me get your back."

A flash of hesitance crossed her face before she slowly rolled over onto her elbows.

I warmed the lotion up between my palms and gently rubbed it into her skin.

"The tide looks like it's heading out. Did you still want to hit the tide pools in Dana Point?"

"Sure," I agreed as I started on her legs, "I think we should hit dinner first though. There's a sushi place up the street that has the best sushi in the state. I can't remember the last time I didn't eat there while I was here."

"Mmmm," the sound sent a bolt of desire through me, "That sounds delicious, actually."

"It's a date then!" I expected her to argue my use of the word "date."

Instead, she patted the sand in front of her, "Your turn. Get your grape smuggling ass over here."

I handed her the bottle of sunscreen and sat down on the sand in front of her. She quickly lubed up my back, leaving blazing trails of lightning along my skin wherever she touched, then commanded me to stand up so she could do my legs.

"Make it quick," I instructed as I rose, "it's hard to hide a boner in this thing."

Porter

I heard her choke on a gasp and the sound of the lotion bottle hitting the sand. I looked down at her over my shoulder and gave her my million-dollar-smile, "I wasn't kidding."

She sprang into action, quickly and sloppily covering my legs from butt cheek to ankle in the creamy protectant.

"Thanks!" I said as I carefully lay down next to her, "I'm glad there weren't any kids walking by for that!"

"You're such a pervert," she accused, "Do you ever talk about anything besides your penis?"

"Not really," I shrugged, "Before now, I've never really met someone who wanted to talk about something else."

"You really need to find better friends then," she mumbled.

I just laughed at her and laid my head down on my arms, prompting her to do the same.

I couldn't tell if her eyes were open behind the lenses of her sunglasses, but the corners of her pouty, paint-free lips were gently curved upward in a contented smile. I told myself that her eyes were open and it was seeing my face that had put that smile there.

A single lock of her reddish-brown hair fell over her forehead. I fought the urge to reach out and brush it back to join the rest that had been tossed over her shoulder.

The dreamy memory of fisting my hands in that hair slammed into me, causing my already-stiff cock to throb against the hard sand beneath me. I squeezed my eyes shut and did my best to think of the least sexy things I could come up with.

It was a trick I used at work to keep myself from getting off too early. I'd make to-do lists, or think about my mailman, or homeless people, and it helped to keep my mind off the task at hand.

It took a bit longer than usual this time, but I finally felt the pressure against my hips begin to lessen and breathed a sigh of relief.

"What's wrong?"

She was *awake!*

"What do you mean?" I asked casually.

"Your face is all screwed up like you have a cramp or something."

David Michael

"Oh, yeah," I agreed, "a cramp. I should've stretched after my workout."

I hoped I sounded more convincing than I thought I did.

The look on her face told me that she didn't believe a word that I said.

"Let's hit the boogie boards in the shallows," she challenged with a grin, "Last one on their board buys dinner!"

She jumped up and snatched both of the foam boards, bolting for the water.

"No fair!" I called after her, "You're cheating!"

I pushed myself up from the towel and ran after her. Cold water was the next-best thing when it came to controlling a hard-on and I was all too happy to let it do its work.

She had dropped the larger of the two boards on the sand just before the water and by the time I made it out there, she was already bobbing up and down on the smaller waves with a childish grin splitting her face from ear-to-ear. It would've been adorable if the board she was leaning on hadn't pushed her tits up to her chin giving me an extraordinary view of her cleavage.

Cold water. Now.

I snatched up the board and ran toward her as fast as I could before dropping to my knees beside her and facing the shore.

"That was cheap and you know it," I said with a playful bump of shoulder against shoulder.

"Call it a handicap," she laughed, "You have longer legs than I do. I needed a head start to make it a fair race."

"A head start I could work with! You stole my board!"

"It was an accident?" She turned her giant doe-eyes on me and tried to look innocent. It was working.

"You should be more careful next time. Someone might mistake your accident for sabotage."

"I'll try to keep that in mind. Thanks in advance for dinner!" She pushed off the sand with her legs right as a wave crashed down on top of my head, propelling me forward off my board and shoving me face-first into the sand beneath the water.

I fought to right myself and spat a mouthful of sand back onto the beach with a cough as the surf receded behind me. Holly

126

was sitting on top of her board a few feet away doubled over with laughter.

"Are you laughing at me, Miss Nash?" I sputtered.

"Oh," she gasped, "you bet your ass I'm laughing at you! That was the funniest damn thing I've seen all week! That's saying a *lot* considering all the time I spend on YouTube! I wish I would've had my camera! I could make some *serious* money off that on *TMZ*!"

Tears were streaming down her face now and, as hard as I tried, I couldn't be mad at her for laughing at my misfortune. Her laughter was like music.

I recovered my board from the tumble of waves behind me and kicked sand at her as I passed her, "Let's go eat. Near death experiences always make me hungry."

"Near death?" she asked as she jogged up next to me, "You were in two feet of water! You were closer to death swimming around out there with the sharks earlier!"

"I wasn't in any danger out there."

"The hell you weren't!" She flopped down on top of her towel and smiled up at me.

"No really," I whispered confidentially, "Can you keep a secret?"

Her face grew serious, "Of course I can."

I crooked a finger at her, motioning for her to lean in closer. I glanced around suspiciously as she moved in and then whispered, "I'm Aquaman."

She burst into a fit of giggles once more and a smile nearly split my face in half. There wasn't a sound on Earth I would rather hear.

"You're such a jackass, Porter!"

She pulled the towel out from under her and began to dry off her hair with the less-sandy side.

"Do we have to change for dinner?" she asked, "Or is this one of those ocean-side catch-of-the-day taco cart-type of places?"

"We'll definitely need some clothes." I glanced down at my speedo, which prominently displayed my bulge.

"Damn," she cursed, "I was hoping I could keep being lazy."

David Michael

I wrapped my towel around my waist and waited for her to finish drying her hair. If she didn't wipe the ocean spray off her tits soon, I'd need more than a towel to make myself acceptable for public presentation.

She finally finished and stood, wrapping the towel around her chest and tucking it under her armpits. She frowned down at our feet.

"What's wrong?" I asked, glancing down as well.

"I didn't get to teach you how to build a *real* sandcastle!"

I laughed and used a finger to gently lift her chin until her eyes met mine.

"I guess that means I get another date."

She didn't flush, but I saw her eyes flick down to my lips as she swallowed hard. I ran a thumb over her mouth before dropping my hand and wrapping my fingers around hers.

"Let's go eat."

I slipped my feet into my flip-flops and grabbed our sand buckets before pulling her with me across the beach toward the car.

"You change first," I handed her the neatly folded clothes from the bottom of the bag and opened the passenger side door for her.

"Turn around, you creeper!"

I pouted out my bottom lip in mock disappointment, "You never let me have any fun!"

I turned and looked back across the beach while she changed. The sun was inching slowly downward toward the western horizon, casting a blinding reflection off the water. In a couple more hours, with any luck, I'd have her wrapped in my arms over the tide pools watching it set.

"Your turn!" she announced

"That was fast!" I held out a hand to help her out of her car.

"I just put my clothes on over my bathing suit. My days of getting naked on the side of the street ended with college."

Well *that* left a lot to the imagination. She had probably just spent a lot of days sunbathing on the beach in between classes, but

Porter

I couldn't help but wonder if she'd ever had to get dressed in a car after a day of more... Entertaining activities.

It was gonna be a bitch to get the damn Speedo off over the hard-on that had reappeared.

"You made me turn around for that?" I asked, incredulous

I sank into the front seat and leaned back, not bothering to wait for her to avert her gaze. When my dick sprang free of the tight swimsuit, she squeaked, threw her hands over her eyes, and turned away from the car screaming swear words into her palms.

"Oh stop," I chastised, "It's not like you've never seen a penis before. We're both adults here."

"Of course I've seen a penis!" she shouted, "I've just never seen *your* penis. In all its rigid glory, even! I have a hard enough time..." She cut herself off.

"A *hard* enough time, what, Holly?" I whispered into her ear. I had managed to get my underwear on and I stood close to her, pressing my hips into her ass. She let out a tiny whimper and involuntarily leaned into me just a tiny bit.

"A hard..." she swallowed, "A hard enough time..."

I wrapped my hands around her hips and pulled her into me. I could feel the shiver that ran through her body.

"Do you have a hard time keeping my naked body out of your head, Holly?" I grinded my shaft against her, "Christ knows I think about yours often enough."

Another moan and her hips swiveled ever so slightly.

"Just one night, Holly. Let's get it out of our systems."

I felt her body go rigid and, after a brief moment of indecision, she stepped forward and turned.

"Food, Porter. We need food. And a table. There needs to be more space. I need a buffer." Her eyes trailed down my chest and stomach to the outline of my erection, "*Now!*"

She turned and walked off in the wrong direction, forcing me to grab my jeans and tee shirt off the front seat. "Holly!" I called after her as I struggled to get my legs into my pants, "Wrong way!"

She turned and came back toward me, not even bothering to laugh as I hopped around on one foot trying to get myself dressed.

I finally got my life together and managed to button my pants. I tugged my shirt down over my head as I power-walked after her.

"Slow down!" I yelled, "We're not in a rush and you're about to sprint past the crosswalk we need!"

She came to an abrupt halt next to the traffic signal pole and mashed the button to cross. I caught up with her right as the light changed and she was off again.

"Holly!" I grabbed her wrist as we hit the opposite corner, "Jesus Christ, woman! I was just flirting! Take a few deep breaths and calm down! If you don't want to sleep with me, I can just jerk off until it turns blue and falls off. It's not a big deal!"

She furrowed her brow at my joke, glaring scarily.

"I'm sorry," I tried, hoping she'd lighten up some, "It was wrong of me to invade your space like that."

"Porter," she sighed, frustrated, "me not wanting to sleep with you is definitely not the problem."

"I'm lost then," I held my hands out to the side, "What the hell was that all about?"

"It's the fact that I *do* want to sleep with you that has me a little freaked out. I haven't wanted someone the way I want you in a *very* long time. I'm just not sure how to deal with it. I'm not sure what I'm supposed to do. I don't even know if it's the *right* thing to do. Or *not* do for that matter. I'm out of my league here and I don't like being out of control. I've been there before and it's not something I ever plan on experiencing again."

"Wait a minute," I put my hands to the sides of my head to keep it from spinning, "Let me get this straight: The reason you won't sleep with me is because you *want* to sleep with me?"

"Yes!" she yelled, "Well, no. It's not that. It's…. It's complicated, Porter."

"I'm gathering that."

"Can we just reset and go get food? I don't want to ruin such a good day with my relationship issues."

I sure as hell wasn't going to let the issue drop, but for the time being, I'd put it on the back burner. It could wait.

Porter

"Sure," I said with a gentle smile, "but only if you'll hold my hand again."

She looked down at my open palm like it was a snake, but slowly slipped her hand into mine.

"See? Not so bad, right?"

"Don't make fun of me, Porter."

"I'm not," I placated, "I'm just saying that we can enjoy each other's company *and* touch without spontaneously combusting."

I wasn't so sure about the last part, but figured I'd throw it in there for good measure. If I *did* burst into flames from the heat I felt when I touched her, at least I could say I died a happy man.

Halfway down the block, I pulled open the glass door to the restaurant and held her hand as she stepped up the single stair. We sat down at a two-top near the door and waited for our server to bring us menus.

"So, what got you into the industry?" I hoped that the topic was a safe one that could lead us back to having a good time together.

"My parents. My mom was an actress and my dad was a producer. Nothing major, but they made ends meet and paid for my schooling. Of course, each of them thought I should follow in their footsteps, but I just didn't have an eye for production and I'm a *terrible* actor. Like, Nicholas Cage bad. So, after several failed attempts in design, makeup, and screenwriting, I finally landed a gig as a secretary at an agency. The boss was impressed with my ability to read people and, after a couple years, I was offered a position as a casting director. I got the shit films for a while, but when my eye started turning nobodies into somebodies, they started handing me the bigger projects. Bigger budget means bigger names. Bigger names mean more connections. Those connections are what I rely on to get A-listers to even glance at a script."

"You're totally a shining example of the American dream then," I said with a smile.

Holly laughed and the tension in my chest loosened. I hadn't realized how bothered I was that she was upset with me until that moment.

"I wouldn't say that," she smiled, "My parents had a lot to do with me getting in at different places. They knew people who knew people. Once I landed the position where I'm at now, it was just a matter of working hard and proving myself."

"That sounds all-too familiar."

"You had much bigger shoes to fill, too. I can only imagine what it was like for you. How old were you when you got into porn?"

"I didn't really get into it on a large scale until I was twenty-three. I had put a few videos up on paid sites before then. My parents never found out about that, luckily. It wouldn't have gone over so well in our house to know that one of the Hale boys was releasing 'cheap' videos on the internet."

She nodded her head as our waiter walked up and set two waters with lemon on the table, "Can I get you anything else to drink?"

"Water's fine for me," I said with a smile.

"I'll take a Sapporo, please."

The guy nodded and walked off to retrieve her beer.

We picked up our menus and browsed through the rolls featured for the month. It didn't take me long to pick three and two appetizers.

When the waiter came back with Holly's beer, she ordered two rolls and no appetizer.

"Hungry?" she asked as she smiled around the neck of her bottle.

"I told you near death experiences make me hungry. I wasn't kidding about that part!"

"And how many near death experiences have you had, Porter?"

She placed her elbows on the table in front of her and stared at me expectantly.

"A few," I shrugged, "I'm a bit of an adrenaline junkie. Usually the trouble I get myself into is relatively safe, but there's always *something* that can go wrong. Not to mention I work with volatile porn directors. I can't even count the number of blunt objects that have been thrown at my head over the course of my career."

"I hardly think a flying dildo counts as 'life threatening'."

I laughed quietly at her joke, "No, the dildos I can take, but the lighting stands are a bit on the painful side. I've gotten good at dodging them though, so don't worry."

"Porn directors really do that? I mean, they take that stuff *that* seriously?"

"Contrary to what the conservative-types in this country would like you to believe, the adult film industry is a nearly a hundred *billion* dollar industry, globally. So yes, directors take it *very* seriously. They stand to make a *lot* of money on a good film. If we're not up to par, they tend to get a little touchy about it."

"I don't think I've ever heard of any director in Hollywood taking things *that* far though. I mean, who the hell would throw the equipment they rely on to make money? Those lights are expensive! I can't imagine they're something that production companies just have lying around in excess."

"Generally speaking, you're right. Most production companies don't. Luckily, or *un*luckily, for me, the companies I work with at my level are generally bigger outfits with a budget to back it up."

"I guess that makes sense, but I still don't see how abusing your talent gets anything done."

"It's just a scare tactic. It works on the new kids. Personally, I've gotten to the point in my career where I'll just walk off set. I don't need that shit in my life and, on the off-chance I have a contract already signed, I can afford to pay for the breach. It hasn't happened in a while, but I think it came pretty close on my last shoot. The director was *super* pissed that I was late. He kinda blew up and tossed hot coffee all over my driver who was posing as my assistant."

She tipped her head to the side and smiled, confused, "Why the hell was your driver posing as your assistant? Don't you *have* an assistant?"

That question did a hell of a job at reminding me that we were both coming from *very* different worlds.

"No," I shook my head as the waiter set my edamame and wantons between us, "I can think of four major porn stars that actually have assistants. And when I say 'major' you should think like, Jenna Jameson level. My dad didn't even have one until the last five years of his career, and then it was because he needed a wrangler, not an assistant—someone to make sure he got to where he needed to be when he needed to be there."

"To be honest, I think that's why most regular movie stars have assistants. I've seen some of those people stumble into my office at ten in the morning either already wasted, or still wasted from the night before. I don't know how they do it. I was in pretty bad shape the day after Preston's party and I didn't even get to drink that much before some oaf walked over the top of me and spilled my martini on my Choos."

Low blow, Nash. Low blow.

"I think we were all a little rough after that party," I said, ignoring her jab, "I think Marco was slipping shit into everyone's drinks."

"I think mine might've been the two bottles of wine I drank *after* the party, but who's to say?"

"Ooooh," I cringed, "Wine hangovers are the worst. My whiskey hangover was pretty shit-tastic, but I'd rather deal with cotton in my head than feeling like I peeled my eyeballs off the carpet. No wine drunks for me!"

She lifted her beer in salute, "I'm trying to refrain."

We picked at the appetizers and stuck to small talk until our sushi arrived. As the waiter placed the fifth and final plate on the table, I saw her cast her gaze around the table.

"Looking for soy sauce?" I asked.

"Yeah. They usually keep it on the table and bring you a little bowl and wasabi."

I shook my head as I stuffed the first massive piece of rice, seaweed, tuna, and carrots in my mouth, "Not here. Each roll comes with its own sauce specific to the roll. It would be an insult to the chef to use soy sauce on it." I swallowed, "Kinda like salting your food as soon as it hits the table without even tasting it first."

"Porter," she picked up a piece of one of her rolls and sniffed it cautiously before stuffing it in her mouth, "I'm gonna ask you this, oh this is delicious, but you can't get offended."

"Oh shit," I set my next bite back down on the plate and waited, "This is gonna be bad, isn't it?"

She swallowed the food in her mouth and pinned me with a serious gaze, "Are you a food snob?"

"Are you kidding?" I wasn't sure that was the question she had meant to ask. Maybe she was a lightweight and the beer had already gone to her head.

"No. I'm dead serious. Are you a foodie?"

I shook my head slowly, not sure of the answer she was looking for, "I wouldn't call myself a food snob, no. I mean, I like fine dining as much as the next guy, but I'm also perfectly fine attending a backyard barbecue in a trailer park. I just have very little manners away from the dinner table, so table manners are where I make up for it. My mom used to kick our asses for bad table manners, so I think it probably just stuck."

"Good," she said, still serious, "because my cooking *sucks*. If I ever invite you to a dinner function, be prepared for boxed food or takeout. You *might* get catered food if I'm feeling particularly celebratory. I am the only person I know who can burn water."

I popped my abandoned piece of sushi in my mouth and smiled at her, "You and Parker would get along in the kitchen then!"

We devoured the rest of our food in silence, mopping up every drop of the sauces with their respective rolls.

"I'm going to hate myself when that rice starts expanding," Holly groaned with a sigh. She leaned back heavily against her chair and rubbed her stomach.

"Let's go walk it off then," I suggested with a smile, "It's low tide, so the pools down at Dana Point should be awesome!"

She nodded her agreement and sipped at her water, "Sounds like a plan."

I waved down the waiter and asked for the check.

"Thank you for dinner," she said once we were back on the sidewalk, "That was probably the best sushi I've had in my life."

"I told you so." She had wrapped her hand in mine again, so I lifted it to my lips and kissed her fingertips, "I wouldn't lie to you."

She met my gaze and, to my surprise, there was none of the wary trepidation that had been there before. Something had changed. There was softness in her eyes that I hadn't seen before.

"For some crazy reason, I believe you when you say that."

I kept myself from wrapping my hand around the back of her head and pulling her in for a kiss—just barely. The urge to dominate her, to own her, to pleasure her, to protect her, swelled inside of me like a tidal wave.

But Holly Nash is not one to be taken. Owned, maybe, but on her terms. I'd make her come to me.

We crossed the street and climbed inside the car.

"Straight south from here. Just look for the pirate ship."

"The pirate ship?"

"Yeah. It's usually moored in the marina. You can't miss it."

"What the hell kind of adventure are you taking me on Porter Hale?"

I flashed her a wicked smile, "The kind you'll never forget."

She put the car in drive and pulled out of the stall. It was only a fifteen-minute drive, and the look on her face when she saw the massive privateer and its five thousand square feet of sail was priceless.

"That, my dear, is the *Spirit of Dana Point*. It's a replica of the ships built during the Revolution. Mostly used for local boy scouts and troubled teens now, but they do the occasional joy ride for the public if you ask really nice."

"It's beautiful! I was expecting a sign in the shape of a pirate ship or a cheesy restaurant or something, not a full-blown real-life boat floating in the bay!"

She pulled into a stall near the ship and almost left the car running in her excitement to get out and see the thing close-up.

We walked along her starboard side from stern to bow, Holly reveling in the beauty of a handcrafted ship, and me reveling in the beauty of her excitement and passion over something so far outside of what I expected her interests to entail.

She named off parts of that ship that I didn't even know *had* names. After my thorough education on the finer points of maritime architecture, we made our way across the parking lot and down a long set of concrete stairs to the coarse sand of the beach.

"This is more my area of expertise," I informed her as we stepped to the edge of the first tide pool, "I don't know a whole lot about sailing, but I can name off hundreds, if not thousands of plants and animals that live in these things."

"I think I could probably give you a run for your money," she winked up at me before crouching down and pointing to the bottom of the pool, "sebastes umbrosus."

I knelt down beside her, nearly dipping my chin into the water to get a better look, "No way! That's a sebastes semicinctus! The umbrosus has white spots and a more pronounced dorsal fin!"

She giggled next to me and nodded her head, "I know. I was just testing you!" She moved her finger a few inches to the left, "Scorpaena gutatta."

I smiled when I spotted the flash of brilliant red as it darted under a rock.

"Strongylocentrotus franciscanus," I said without pointing.

"The red sea urchin. Watch out for those little bastards," she held her fingers a few inches apart, "nothing like a couple dozen three inch spines buried in your foot to ruin a day at the beach! Anthopleura elegantissima."

I had almost missed the tiny bed of brilliant magenta and green anemones, "You've got a pretty good eye."

"Tide pools fascinated me as a kid. The fact that they change every day and each one holds such an insanely diverse ecosystem just enthralled me. I used to sit at the edge of them until the tide came back in and my parents made me move. I always wanted to know where all the animals went when they weren't landlocked anymore and what caused them to climb down into these holes in the first place."

I pushed myself up from the edge of the rocky depression, "First one to find a Ruby Octopus gets to pick the movie we watch on our next date!"

I took off running before she even had a chance to get herself upright. I had already spotted a pool big enough to make it likely that there would be one of the elusive octopi in it and knew I had the contest in the bag. I skidded to a halt at the edge of the eight by four foot cauldron in the ground and scanned the bottom for the telltale signs of the expert practitioner of crypsis.

Thanks to the chromatophores in their skin, they can instantly change to any shade of red, brown, orange, black, or yellow they need in order to blend into their surroundings. They also have expert control of the papillae, the small bumps on their skin, and can mimic textures ranging from smooth to spikey, rendering them nearly invisible.

"I win!" she cried from a few yards to the south of me.

I cursed under my breath and headed her direction to confirm her success.

"You're full of shit," I announced after surveying her pool.

"Are you kidding me right now?" she had her hands on her hips and a single eyebrow lifted.

I scanned the pool again, looking more closely for an eyeball or a stray tentacle that tended to give the creatures away.

"I'm still not seeing anything."

She let out a derisive snort and bent down close to the surface.

"I'm disappointed in you, Porter!" She quickly dipped a hand into the pool, poking the wall nearest her. Much to my dismay, it bloomed to a brilliant shade of red and released a small cloud of black ink as the adolescent octopus shot to the opposite wall and puffed up in an attempt to scare her off.

"Son of a bitch," I grumbled, "You're gonna make me watch a chick flick, aren't you?"

"There's a definite possibility," she teased, "Not because I want to watch it, but because you *don't*."

I rolled my eyes and rose from the edge of the now-murky tide pool. I had spotted a rocky ledge that butted up to the surf and wanted to be on top of it when the sun set. I had a high level of certainty that she would follow me without me having to say anything, so I headed across the sand, carefully skirting tide pools in the ever-dimming light.

Holly didn't disappoint.

She took my offered hand and joined me on the flat surface of the short, narrow ledge.

As we stood there, her hand still in mine, we looked out over the Pacific in silence as the sun sank toward the distant horizon. The thin wisps of cloud still lingering in the sky flamed orange and pink, bathing us, and our slice of heaven, in its rose-gold glow.

The constant spray of the surf crashing against the rocks at our feet chilled the summer air and surrounded us with its briny scent. As the sun finally touched on the horizon, its golden reflection stretched toward us like a pathway we could follow to the end of the Earth and beyond.

Holly stepped into my side and shivered slightly. I wrapped my arms around her and pulled her close to my chest, using my own body heat to help keep her warm.

Neither of us said a word as we stood there watching the last of the day's light disappear below the horizon.

I rested my chin on top of her head and tried not to think about the beast inside of me that she had awakened. I could feel it shifting around and knew it was only a matter of time before it was fully alert and took control. I wanted to enjoy the time we had together before that happened and we were forced to go our separate ways.

She sighed heavily and relaxed into me, folding her hands over the top of mine.

Twilight had officially fallen over California and the tide was slowly making its way back up the shoreline. If we didn't move soon, we'd be stuck on the rock and our only option would be to wade through the shallows back to dry land.

"We should get back up to the car," I didn't loosen my hold at all, "before the tide comes in."

She nodded her head, but didn't say anything. We stood there a few moments longer before she finally dropped her arms and took a half step forward.

David Michael

I wasn't prepared for the nakedness I felt without her pressed into me. Alarms went off in my head, warning me to cut ties and run while I could, but the next words out of her mouth silenced them.

Four words from her and I was practically on my knees ready to drop rose petals on the ground she walked on.

"Come home with me."

Sixteen
Holly

As soon as the words left my mouth a knot of terror formed in my stomach. An invisible steel band clamped down around my chest making it hard to breathe and I couldn't do anything but stare at him, waiting for a response.

I, Holly Nash, had just asked a porn star to come home with me.

What if he said no? What if he laughed at me? Or worse, what if he said *yes*?

Porter just stood there, frozen, for what seemed like an eternity.

Finally, he smiled softly and without a word, reached his hand toward me.

This is really happening.

The excitement that rushed through me overshadowed the terror and I began to breathe again.

Of its own accord, my own hand slid into his and my legs robotically carried me along beside him back to the car.

I drove on autopilot the entire way back into Los Angeles. I couldn't spare any focus for the road since every ounce of my willpower was being devoted to fighting off the panic attack that threatened to overtake me.

The silence between us was awkward. I wasn't able to form words and no hint of Porter's usual easygoing demeanor was present. He stared straight ahead, didn't touch the stereo, and never took his hand off of mine.

I pulled into my driveway and shut off the ignition. We both sat there like nervous teenagers outside a cheap motel on prom night.

"I need wine," I blurted as I opened my door and practically jumped out of the car.

He followed suit, a little more calmly than I had, and we made our way up the walkway to the front door.

My anxiety spiked as my trembling hand slid the key into the lock and a vision of Porter sliding into me in the same way flashed through my mind's eye.

I bolted for the kitchen as soon as the door swung open, trusting that Porter would have the sense to close it behind us. Two of my largest wine glasses were filled to the brim with merlot before he even made his way into the kitchen.

I downed half of mine in one breath and refilled it as he calmly lifted his own glass and sipped at it. The huge dose of wine did wonders for my nerves and reminded me to take a deep breath. My hands steadied as I did so and the terror I felt slowly taking the reins again gave way to a giddy excitement. The heat from the wine spread through my stomach and mixed with the warmth that had begun to spread throughout me at the prospect of having Porter in my house.

"Feel better?" he asked when I had finally stopped quivering.

"A bit," I took a more controlled sip of my wine.

"This can all happen at your pace, Holly. I'm not going to let you do anything you're not one hundred percent on-board with."

The soft reassurance further suppressed any doubts I felt and my confidence in my invitation began to rise. The fact that Porter Hale could stand in my kitchen with a raging hard-on and tell me that the ball was in my court flipped a switch inside me and my walls started coming down.

I took another long swallow from my glass before setting it down on the counter and taking a step toward him. I reached up with one hand and ran a thumb over the sexy stubble on his jaw. I couldn't help but smile at the anticipation I could see burning in his eyes. My other hand went to his groin, pressing his impressive anatomy against my palm and slowly rubbing my way along its length.

"It's been a *long* time for me, Porter. One step at a time is all I can handle."

I could feel the warmth of his arousal as I reached the head, causing it to jump beneath my fingers. He hissed a breath through his teeth and set his own wine glass down on the counter beside mine.

Before I could register what was happening, his strong fingers were wrapped in my hair, holding my head in place as his lips crushed down on mine like a starving man before a feast. He pressed his way into my mouth, taking all I was willing to give. I could feel him tasting, sampling, exploring, and savoring me. I was powerless to stop him, but there wasn't a single part of me that wanted to. I opened for him and let him ravish me with his mouth.

About the time I began to see stars, his heated kisses finally gave way to gentleness. Sated, he planted one last kiss on my jaw and stepped away panting.

Without the support of his hands on my head, I had to lean against the counter or risk collapsing to the floor as the heady high of my passion threatened to topple me.

"That was," I gasped, "intense."

"I'm sorry I lost control. I needed to taste you, Holly. From the first moment I laid eyes on you, I've wanted to do that. I swear to you that whatever happens tonight, you're in control from here on out."

The idea of having Porter at my command shot a tongue of heat through my sex. The bikini bottoms I still wore beneath my pants were soaked and it wasn't from the ocean.

A spot of wetness had also appeared at the end of the bulge in Porter's jeans. I had the sudden, uncontrollable urge to taste him as well.

I took him by the hand and led him from the kitchen, abandoning the half-full glasses of wine.

Butterflies the size of kittens rioted in my stomach. They became more frantic with each step we took toward my bedroom door until I was sure that if I opened my mouth they'd come fluttering out.

The door closed behind us with a gentle click and I led him over to the bed, guided only by the dim light filtering through my windows from the alley behind my house.

I squeaked in surprise as his powerful arms scooped me off my feet and my heart hammered in my chest as he gently lay me down on the bed. He stood over me, staring as if he couldn't believe what he was seeing. I stared right back, taking in every inch of his lean, predatory body. His tee shirt stretched with each rapid, heaving breath he took and I knew at that moment that he was just as impatient for what was about to happen as I was.

Porter lowered himself onto the bed beside me and softly kissed my lips. He peppered gentle whispers of flesh-on-flesh along my jaw and neck then down to my collarbone. I closed my eyes and pushed every last thought out of my head. I didn't want to think about it, I just wanted to *feel* it; to feel *him*.

One of his huge hands came down on my waist and skirted its way beneath my shirt. The feeling of his strong fingers trailing across my hip bone sent my nervous system into overdrive. Every inch of my body, inside and out, tingled with the electricity of his touch. The path he traced over the flesh between my hip and my ribs blazed to life and shot pulses of need straight to the center of me.

My breath hitched as his fingers slid under the bikini top and tenderly massaged the overly sensitive flesh of my breast. He growled deep in his chest as his hips pressed forward and crushed his erection into my thigh.

His exploration finally landed on my nipple and I moaned and arched my back as he gently took the peaked nub between his thumb and forefinger. A mixture of color and shadow burst before my eyes and I knew that I was going to climax before he even made his way south of the border.

His hips were now grinding against me steadily as he slowly worked my nipple. His mouth came down on mine and I opened for him once more, allowing him to pull the flavors from my mouth with his tongue. He wanted to taste me, to know me, to consume me. I could feel it in the way he made sure to explore every inch.

I squeezed my thighs together in an attempt to alleviate some of the ache that had built up between them, but the sensation had the opposite effect. The whisper of cotton over my clitoris, when combined with the sensations Porter's body provided, sent me over the edge. I came hard for him.

The sound of my release triggered something inside of him and his actions became more urgent—more desperate.

His hand shot out of my shirt and tugged at the button on my jeans as he sat up and removed his shirt with his free hand.

"I want to taste you, Holly. I want to swallow you down and have you inside me. May I taste you?" The words were controlled and breathy, as if it took everything he had not to shout them at me.

"Please," I begged.

That one word was all the encouragement he needed.

I heard the button from my jeans land somewhere across the room and he tugged the denim off my legs with such force that I was nearly dragged to the floor with them. He shoved the strip of bikini to the side and took me to the edge once more.

When his mouth crushed down on my sex and my world flew apart, I can't remember what words flew out of my mouth. All I recall were the groans of approval as my orgasm flooded out of me and into Porter. He pressed his mouth to me, nursing every last bit as if it were the only thing on the planet that could sustain him. His tongue lapped at me as he gasped for breath and fought to control himself. I could feel him vibrating with the force of his restraint.

When I came down from the high he had given me, I wasted no time in begging for another. My entire body was alive in a way I had never experienced. Porter had awakened something inside me. Something powerful and primal flowed through me every time he touched me.

"I can't wait anymore," I moaned, "I want you inside me, Porter."

He groaned and trailed a finger along my slit, "You're even more beautiful than I had imagined, Holly."

145

He pushed the bikini top up over my breasts and brought his mouth down on my nipple as I struggled to remove it the rest of the way. He gently sucked the soft pink bud into his mouth and flicked his tongue over it, causing it to harden. At the same moment, he slid a single finger into me, filling a fraction of the space that begged to be occupied.

"Porter," I needed everything he had to offer and my voice did nothing to hide my desire, "Porter, please."

I could feel another orgasm building inside me as his tongue and teeth worked my nipple hungrily and his thumb traced circles over my clit as another finger slid into me all the way to the knuckle.

He could feel it building, too.

His mouth and fingers massaged me in perfect time with each other. He ruthlessly drove me back to the edge and kept me hanging there with his relentless pace. He slid another finger into me without breaking his rhythm and I shattered yet again.

Porter continued his assault on my senses even as the walls of my vagina clamped down around his hand, grabbing at him like a drowning man would a life preserver.

The fog that filled my brain and blurred my vision was more stubborn to dissipate than those of my previous orgasms. I was rendered incapable of speech by the force of the climax and the only way I could communicate what my body wanted was to moan and mewl, mutely begging him to fill me completely. To join with me in the only way he hadn't yet.

He pulled his fingers out of me suddenly, leaving me empty and gasping for breath.

"Condom," he snapped.

What?

I moaned in hazy response.

"Holly!" the word was harsh and cleared enough of the cotton in my brain that I could follow what he said next, "I need a condom. *Now!*"

"I..." I tried to remember what a condom was, "I don't think I have any of those."

"Fuck!" he cursed, so loudly that I jumped.

Porter

As the reality of the situation sank in, guilt began to worm its way around in my stomach. I couldn't leave him like that.

I pushed myself up into a sitting position and slowly crawled to the foot of the bed where he stood watching me. I reached a shockingly confident hand toward his belt. His exposed abdomen distracted me before I could be bothered to fight with his belt.

I splayed my fingers over the smooth, solid surface just above the waist of his jeans. The muscle was hard, but the skin there was so soft to the touch. I traced a single finger down the deep groove to one side of the rippling six-pack before me. His breath hitched and the muscles in his stomach tightened as the tip of my finger dipped into his pants.

Faster than I'd ever seen anyone move before, he had his belt off and his fly open. I could see the outline of his shaft through his underwear and felt a dull, aching throb begin to pulse inside of me.

Simply going down on him wasn't going to quench the thirst my body had for him. I would have him buried inside of me before the night was through—one way or another.

Fair is fair though, and a little foreplay never hurt anything.

I reached forward, parting the opening to his pants even further and tugging them down his hips.

Inch after inch of his massive dick was revealed to me beneath the thin veil of his cotton boxer-briefs. When it finally sprang free of the denim, he groaned in relief and dropped his head back so that he was looking up at the ceiling.

I could now see the outline of the huge head that crowned his thick shaft. It was only a couple inches smaller in diameter than my wrist. A brief moment of panic shot through me as I wondered how I would fit it inside of me. I quickly pushed the thought aside and focused on the task at hand.

My hand had started trembling again as I reached forward to take hold of him.

I hooked a finger in either side of the elastic band and pulled downward, slowly revealing what was left to see of his body. I slowly moved my fingers together as the undergarment dropped until my fingers framed the bulk of his stiff cock, gently stroking the sensitive skin as I finished unveiling his sex.

I traced the tip of my finger around the massive tip. The entire length of him jumped beneath my hand and a small drop of lubricant slid out of his slit and onto my finger.

I glanced up and met his intense gaze. He had been watching me explore his body. I raised my finger, slick with his arousal, and slid it between my lips without breaking eye contact.

He moaned deep in his chest and his cock jumped again, pulling my attention back to pleasing him. I wrapped my fingers around him and slowly pumped from base to head and back before leaning forward and lapping at the sweet nectar that had beaded at the tip.

Porter hissed a sharp breath through his teeth at the delicate contact of my warm tongue with his now-throbbing penis.

I hesitated a moment with my mouth half open.

"I'm clean. I have to get tested once a month."

It only took me a moment to realize he had mistaken my hesitance for fear of disease.

"I was just considering how I was going to fit it inside of me," I whispered with a wink.

Before he could say anything else or my brain could talk me out of going forward, I opened my mouth as far as I could and impaled my throat on his shaft.

"Oh my..." he groaned, tensing his entire body, "*Fuck!*"

I sealed my lips around him and began a slow, steady assault on his senses. Each time the end of his length pressed against my tonsils, I gagged just a little bit, causing him to moan in ecstasy and gently push his hips forward before I could draw myself off him again. When I came to the end, I took a deep breath through my nose and swirled my tongue around the underside of his head. I made sure to pay special attention to the bundle of nerves on the bottom of his shaft.

"God, Holly," his hands rested gently on top of my head as I continued to work him at my own pace, "You feel so good."

I could feel his fingers slowly tightening on my hair and knew he was getting close.

Porter

The idea of him finishing without being inside of me the way I wanted made my vagina throb in protest. I continued to take him deeper and deeper into my throat with each repetition and, to alleviate the need that had built itself into an all-consuming desire, reached down to plunge to of my own fingers inside me.

I came almost instantly, moaning around the flesh that filled my mouth and drawing another primal groan of satisfaction out of Porter.

"Holly," his voice had gone up an octave and he was practically pulling my hair out of my scalp, "I'm gonna..."

I popped my mouth off of him before he could finish, "No you're not. You're clean, I'm clean, and I'm on birth control. We can buy condoms tomorrow."

I leapt at him, wrapping my legs around his hips and causing him to stumble backwards. I crushed my mouth down on his as he tried to catch his balance. He took two more steps backwards and his back met with the door, jolting us both to the bone.

He stepped out of his jeans and underwear still wrapped around his ankles.

I nipped at his bottom lip and used my legs around his waist to leverage myself up and down, occasionally bringing my swollen, super-heated sex in contact with his own throbbing arousal.

He snarled in time with the contact, crushing my ass with his powerful hands more fiercely with each thrust.

"If you're sure, Holly, I need to be inside of you *now*. I can't wait anymore. I've been thinking about nothing else for weeks and being this close is a cruel form of torture."

I licked the lip I had bitten and smiled down at him, "I'm sure."

I lowered my feet to the floor and placed a hand on his chest for a brief moment before turning and walking back to the foot of the bed. I tugged at the strings of the bikini bottoms letting them fall to the floor before I bent over the edge of the bed and spread my legs.

I tossed my hair over my shoulder and smiled back at him.

He pushed away from the door and closed the space between us in two long, predatory strides. He moved like a lion about to pounce on his prey.

Before he reached me, he stopped short and dropped to his knees, planting one hand on either of my ass cheeks and dipping his head between my thighs.

As he worked his tongue into my slit, another orgasm began to build throughout my entire body. It was going to be a big one.

"Porter," I panted, "you need to get inside me right fucking now. I can't come again without feeling you. I don't have enough left in me to keep going like this."

"Mmmm," he hummed against my sex before rising from his knees, "I live to serve."

Porter positioned his hips behind me, spreading the fingers of one hand across my back. He used his other hand to guide himself to my entrance and we both quivered in anticipation and arousal as he slid it from the bottom of my slit to the top, gently slapping the head against my clit before slowly guiding it deeper into my folds.

My body tensed involuntarily, bracing for the penetration.

He was a porn star, for crying out loud. I had known all along he wouldn't be gentle about it just because I hadn't had sex since Jesus had walked the Earth.

"Holly," his voice was low and comforting, "relax."

He pressed his hips forward, but only enough to cause pressure against the tight muscles there. Both hands were now on my lower back, slowly tracing gentle circles over the tense muscles there and down over the mounds of my ass.

He hadn't moved an inch, but maintained a constant pressure against me and slowly, achingly so, inched his way inside me. As his head slipped fully inside me, the stretching sensation eased and I felt myself relax even further. I could feel his hands trembling against my back from the exertion of his self-control.

He wanted to bury himself in me. I could feel the barely contained energy of his desire pulsing through him as if it were my own.

Porter

I used my arms to push myself back into him, gritting my teeth as he filled me until I thought I would burst. Then he filled me even more.

When my ass finally came flush with his hips, we both breathed a sigh of relief. He leaned all the way forward, pressing his stomach and chest against my back, and placed gentle kisses along the back of my neck. My pussy throbbed around him, adjusting to the intrusion.

"You feel so good, Holly," he planted a kiss at the base of my neck. "You smell good. You taste good. You look," he paused and growled as his cock pulsed inside of me, "you look like a goddess."

He pulled out of me a couple of inches and slowly pressed back in to the hilt. He did this several times; all the while trailing kisses down my spine as he slowly made his way back to an upright position.

By the time he was vertical again, he had quickened his pace and I had loosened up enough to enjoy the sensation of having him inside of me. There was a wonderful sense of fullness that I had forgotten accompanied sex and it ushered the swell of the powerful release that was still building inside of me.

Porter's powerful hands gripped my hips, his fingers digging into the flesh there, as he drove himself into me again and again. With each thrust, waves of passion rolled through me. My brain could no longer distinguish which one of us was vocalizing their pleasure. My vision went hazy as my body clamped down around him in preparation for yet another release.

I screamed his name as I came, long and hard, but he never faltered. He maintained the brutal pace of our lovemaking, prolonging my pleasure and keeping me at the peak until my throat hurt from my cries of ecstasy.

The roar that ripped out of him as he thrust into me one final time probably woke my neighbors, but I couldn't find it in me to care. He collapsed on top of me and we rolled onto our sides with him slowly softening inside of me.

Sweaty and panting, we both lie there weak and exhausted until we drifted off to sleep.

David Michael

The last thing I remember was Porter intertwining his fingers with mine and pulling me into his chest.

I knew I'd be safe there.

Seventeen
Porter

The soft glow of pre-dawn crept lazily into the room, tinting the whole world with its calming blue hues. My muscles ached and my arm was asleep, but I couldn't bring myself to disturb her.

Holly Nash was asleep next to me and she looked absolutely stunning.

Her hair flowed over my arm and down her back, begging me to reach out and stroke it. Her scent clung to me like a dark, flowery perfume. If I closed my eyes and held my breath, I could still taste her on my tongue.

No woman had ever had that effect on me. Of all the women I had gone through in my life, Holly Nash was the only one who had ever lingered so completely.

Too many red flags, Hale. Get out before it's too late.

I ignored the nagging voice of reason in my head and reached out to stroke her beautiful hair. It was so much softer than I had dreamed. I ran my hand down its entire length, reliving the experience of having it fisted in my fingers the night before.

The memory immediately stiffened me against her back, causing her to stir.

"Mmm," she grumbled, "What time is it?"

"Early," I replied, "You should go back to sleep."

"Okay."

Holly snuggled back into me, pressing herself even tighter against me and wiggling her hips, working my hard-on into her crack.

She flipped over suddenly, fully awake.

"Were you watching me sleep?"

I laughed and trailed my index finger down her perfect nose, "Yes."

Her mouth opened and closed a couple times and she furrowed her brow for just a moment before smiling widely, "Okay."

She worked her hand down between us and gave my cock a squeeze, "Was he watching me, too?"

I sighed, "He was. Sadly, since he only has one eye, his depth perception is a little off and I'm afraid he might've bumped into you. He says he's sorry."

She clicked her tongue disapprovingly, "Well, that's not very polite of him."

"He can be a bit of a bastard sometimes. I beat him for it fairly often. It doesn't seem to do any good though."

"Well," she pressed her lips into a firm line, trying not to smile, "maybe we should try a different kind of punishment then. I hear asphyxiation is a terrible experience."

I managed to maintain my straight face by biting down on the inside of my cheek, "He's a kinky bastard. Knowing him, he'd probably like it."

"We won't know until we try, right?"

She gave my now-twitching anatomy another squeeze and smiled wickedly as she pushed me onto my back and knelt over me, gently rubbing her hot pussy along its length.

"Hold your breath, little buddy," I stage whispered to my penis, making her laugh as she plunged herself down on top of me.

The pulsing of her laughter gripped me like a vice as she slowly lifted herself off of me and lowered herself back down again. The sensation, along with the experience of watching her use me for her pleasure, nearly sent me over the edge.

"Turn around and lean forward," I instructed, "I want to watch while you fuck me."

She followed my directions expertly, turning one hundred and eighty degrees without pulling me out of her, and continued to ride me.

I reached up and fisted my hand in her hair, gently pulling her back, and her cadence changed completely.

154

She was no longer worried about the soft and gentle enjoyment of our morning session; she rammed herself down into my hips, undoubtedly jamming the tip of my cock into her cervix as evidenced by the quiet yelp.

She applied a little bit of caution with the next thrust but didn't slow down at all. I almost regretted telling her to turn around as I imagined her tits bouncing beautifully with each thrust.

"Oh, fuck yeah," I groaned as she came down on my shaft and swiveled her hips.

"Holly!" the bedroom door burst open and a tiny little redhead burst through it, "If you're not dead I'm going to—holy mother of God!"

Holly was off me and wrapped up in the sheet before I could even register what was happening.

"Becks!" she screamed, "What the hell are you doing here?"

Becks' eyes were glued to my hard-on as she stood there with her mouth hanging open and her eyes wide in shock.

Holly rushed over to her and snapped her fingers in front of her face, breaking the spell my penis had cast on her.

"The last thing I heard from you was a picture of you holding some dude's underwear! You didn't respond to the forty-two million texts I've sent since then and you didn't answer any of my calls. Or Mitch's for that matter. We thought you were dead or something!"

"Clearly, I'm not dead, Becks! Thanks for checking on me, now could you please get the hell out of my house?"

Holly was blushing a brilliant shade of red that I could make out even in the dim light and it took everything I had not to laugh at her.

"Nice to meet you, Becks!" I called as she turned to leave, earning me a death glare from Holly.

"Nice to meet you, Ryder!" she tossed over her shoulder as Holly slammed the door behind her.

"She seems like a nice girl," I smiled up at a very flustered Holly, "and she obviously has superb taste in porn."

"Shut up, Porter!" Holly pulled a long tee shirt over her head, covering up all of my favorite parts, "My best friend just walked in on me riding a porn star like a pony. Now isn't really a good time to talk about her watching you have sex while she touches herself. The thought of her doing that while replaying what she just saw creeps me out."

She slipped a pair of boy shorts on under the tee shirt and tossed my boxer-briefs at me. I just left them lying where they landed on my chest and grinned at her with my arms folded behind my head. I was still rock-hard and I had hopes that she would realize it and finish what she had started.

No such luck. She opened the door and stormed out into the hallway, leaving me high and mostly dry.

"What the hell are you doing?" I heard her screech from somewhere down the hall. I couldn't hear the response, but the next words out of her mouth fired up my curiosity.

"He doesn't need fucking breakfast!"

I slid my underwear on, doing my best to conceal my giant boner, and slipped out of bed. I padded my way down the hallway as quietly as I could to try and get a sneak peek at what I was missing.

I had only made it a few steps outside the bedroom when the smell of sausage and eggs hit me.

As I rounded the corner into the kitchen, Holly spun and snapped at me, "Tell this stubborn bitch that you don't need breakfast!"

My stomach growled loudly at that exact moment, announcing that I did actually need breakfast.

I glanced down at my bellybutton and back to her, "The boss has spoken. A man's stomach is second in command only to his penis. If both are not satisfied, I am incapable of thinking for myself." I smiled at Becks who was clearly trying not to laugh while she scrambled eggs in a frying pan, "Food me, woman!"

"You two are insufferable!" Holly clutched the mug of coffee she had procured and stomped out of the kitchen.

"Is she always like this in the mornings?" I asked as I took the empty mug Becks offered.

"I've seen worse," she shrugged, "She'll get over it. I just don't recommend trying to talk to her until she's had a cup of coffee or two. She might throw something at your head."

"Noted," I poured myself a cup of the steaming liquid, "Anything else I should be aware of that may cause serious bodily injury?"

Becks thought for a moment before answering, "Yeah, actually. Me. You hurt her, I *will* kill you."

There wasn't a doubt in my mind as to the seriousness of her threat. I nodded my agreement and she nodded back. We had a deal.

"Now go find some clothes. Your nakedness is dickstracting."

"Dickstracting? Really?"

"Yes. Now go."

Instead of following her instructions and finding my clothes, I chose to try my luck dickstracting Holly.

"I'm immune," she announced before I even made it to the couch, "go put your pants on."

"How do you know you're immune?" I asked, "You didn't even look up from your coffee mug!"

She met my eyes, gave me a cursory once-over from head to toe and back, then said with a shrug, "Yep. Still immune."

"This isn't over," I grumbled as I made my way back to the bedroom.

When I rejoined them at the bar-style counter that Holly used as a dining table a few minutes later, a sudden hush fell over the room and they were both overly interested in their food.

"You two weren't talking about me while I wasn't here to defend myself, were you?"

"No," Holly said, too quickly.

"Yes," Becks answered at the same time.

"And the truth shall set you free," I muttered as I sat down in front of my plate.

"I brought mimoooooosa's!" The door slammed shut and a flamboyant man laden with grocery bags came around the corner a moment later.

"Becks! What the hell?" Holly asked accusingly.

"Oh! Holly, I didn't know you had company!" he announced unconvincingly, "Who's your friend?"

"Mitch you know damn good and well who my friend is. And we have work today. We're not drinking four bottles of champagne this early in the morning."

"Ryder," Mitch nodded to me, "Did you get your underwear back?"

"I did."

Word travels fast in this group.

"Damn," he had the grace to look crestfallen, "Just my luck."

Mitch turned his attention to his boss, "Holly, we work in Hollywood and your schedule is relatively clear for the day. Just call in drunk. We can reschedule anything semi-important and between the two of us, we should be able to field any emails from here."

The cork came off the first bottle with a pop causing Becks to clap and bounce on her stool with excitement.

"Yaaaaaay! Day drinking with my two besties!" she flashed me a Cheshire grin, "And a porn star."

"Not a porn star," I corrected, clouding her face with confusion, "*the* porn star."

Mitch cackled from the kitchen, Holly choked on the mouthful of eggs she had just shoveled in, and Becks took the comment in stride, "Sorry, *the* porn star. Do you want me to refer to you as 'Your Majesty' as well?"

I rolled my eyes upward and tapped a finger on my chin, feigning thoughtfulness, "I prefer 'Your Holy Sexiness' but I'll leave it up to you."

"Don't encourage them, Porter."

"Oh, honey," Mitch crooned as he placed four champagne flutes at the end of the bar, "encourage us all you want. It makes it easier to look at your ass when we don't have to think about talking to you."

"Mitch!" Holly chastised with a glare, "You're such a slut!"

"I know," he countered with a shrug, "and you love me for it."

"Do I?" Holly grumbled as she scooped up the last of her eggs.

"Of course you do," Mitch said matter-of-factly, "Doesn't she, Becks?"

"She sure does, Love Muffin. And so do I." She raised her glass to him in a toast to Mitch's inability to think about anything but sex.

"Are there always this many people in your house in the morning?" I whispered to Holly.

"No," she glared accusingly at them, "only when Becks walks in on me having sex and texts Mitch to come over so he doesn't miss out on my humiliation."

"I see," I stuffed the last sausage link on my plate into my mouth and gathered our dishes, "Let's make it worth their time then."

"Porter..."

I walked into the kitchen before she could protest and set the dishes in the sink. I then made my way back to the bedroom with her hot on my heels.

"Porter, what are you doing?"

"Nothing," I replied innocently as I took my shirt off once again, "go back to your mimosa. Give me a minute."

"I don't like the look in your eyes. This isn't going to end well, is it?"

"Holly," I put my hands on her shoulders, "go drink your juice and call into work. If this goes the way I think it will, we'll have plenty of time to finish what we started this morning without anymore interruptions."

She huffed out a breath and crossed herself, "God help me."

Once I was alone, I quickly stripped down and turned the shower on in the master bathroom, hoping the water was loud enough for them to hear down the hall. Mitch and Becks would undoubtedly work themselves into a frenzy over imagining me wet and naked.

I stepped under the hot spray and let it wash away the sweat of the day before. I was a little bit sad about washing the smell of Holly off me, but it was for the greater good. Besides, if I had my way, I'd be covered in it again very soon.

I stepped out of the shower onto the bathmat and smiled at my reflection in the mirror.

"This is gonna be good."

The thought of having Holly on top of me again had me hard as a rock once more and I pulled the hand towel from the stainless steel holder beside the sink. I dropped it onto my shaft, turning myself into a living towel rack and headed back for the living room.

Soaking wet from head to toe and wearing nothing but a towel barely big enough to cover my groin, I made my entrance, "Holly, could you give me a hand?"

All three heads turned at the sound of my voice and identical expressions covered their faces. Mitch even managed to drop his champagne flute, shattering it on the hardwood floor and spraying their feet with fizzy orange juice.

"I couldn't find the towels," I put my hands on my hips and gave them my best innocent face, "and our interrupted session this morning has caused a bit of a problem."

Holly was the first to get her senses back and she leapt from the couch, practically sprinting past me to a closet at the end of the hall. She shoved a folded towel into my arms and tried her hardest to control the flush I could see working its way up her neck.

I tossed it around my neck and smiled at her, "Thanks!"

I quick jerk of my hips had the smaller towel sliding off my still-stiff cock and falling to the floor in a heap. I ignored it and had to bite my tongue to keep from laughing when Mitch squealed from his perch on the couch and Becks covered her eyes with her hands and shook her head. I was almost certain she was peeking through the cracks of her fingers. Holly just fidgeted, unsure of how to respond.

I turned to return to the bedroom and dry off, bending to retrieve the scrap of cloth I had covered myself with and giving Mitch the show of his life in the process. I heard a strangled gurgling sound come from his throat before I straightened and left the room with a mischievous grin on my face.

Holly chased me into the bedroom and I used her body to close the door behind her.

"What the hell was *that* all about?" she hissed.

"We're going to let them use their imaginations to fill in the holes about what's going on behind this door. If they have a single shred of dignity between them, they'll slip out and let us do our business in peace," I whispered.

"I don't think-"

"Yeah," I groaned too loudly, "do that with your tongue again. Fuck!"

"Porter," she tried to interrupt my performance, "this isn't-"

"God! I love the way you feel around me!"

Holly rolled her eyes and pushed firmly on my chest, forcing me to take a step backwards, "They're not going to leave, Porter. If anything, they're going to set up a picnic outside the bedroom door and get wasted while they eavesdrop."

"We are not!" their voices chimed in unison from the hallway outside the door.

Holly turned the knob and swung the door open to reveal the two of them camped out on either side of the hall with a bottle of champagne and a gallon of orange juice between them.

They smiled up at us unabashedly.

"I guess that's what I get for giving you the benefit of the doubt," I said through gritted teeth as I wrapped the towel around my waist and moved to find my clothes.

"We lost our last communal shred of dignity a few years ago," Becks proclaimed as she took a sip of her mimosa.

"I think we left it somewhere in WeHo," Mitch clarified, "Those clubs have a way of gobbling up whatever self-respect you have."

"Why am I still friends with you two?" Holly asked as she stepped over their pow-wow and went back into the living room.

"The two of you are the biggest cock blockers ever," I accused before kicking the door shut in their faces.

I could hear their laughter even as they made their way down the hall to rejoin Holly.

David Michael

If I had known what that morning would do to the rest of my life, I might've done things differently.

Looking back on it now, I'm glad I didn't.

Eighteen
Holly

"Has it really been three months?" Porter asked groggily.

"Mmhmm," I responded as I kissed his neck, "Three months ago today was the first time we had sex."

"I think I like the sex even better now," he still hadn't moved a muscle since I had rolled off of him.

"I'm pretty sure I can agree with that statement. My furniture on the other hand," I surveyed the wreckage of what had once been a lamp and an end table, "not so much. We really need to work on our landings."

"I'll put it on the to-do list."

Those were my favorite moments. Post-sex pillow talk with Porter Hale was an experience in and of itself. He was usually the one talking everyone's ear off, so I cherished the moments when I had the upper hand and his brain was still disconnected from the rest of his body.

"How'd your audition go today?" I asked as I traced a finger down his bare chest. We were lying on the living room floor after barely making it inside with our clothes on.

"It went well, I think. But in the long run, we both know it's going to come down to politics."

I knew he was right and hated it. He had real talent and some serious devotion to his craft. We spent a good portion of our time together going over lines and blocking out his auditions, so I had seen first-hand what he could do. Unfortunately, most production companies couldn't see past the horrendous mess that would come with casting a porn star in a mainstream film.

David Michael

"It's a numbers game, Porter," the line felt rehearsed with how many times I'd had the same conversation with Becks over the years, "You just have to keep at it. You'll get a role eventually."

"I know," he sighed, "I think I'm going to officially announce my retirement. It can't hurt anything, right?"

I knew exactly what kind of PR nightmare it would create for him, but if he was serious about making it in the mainstream industry, it was a good move.

"I think it's been long enough that people won't really be surprised by it," I said, "I think it's a good move for your career, to be honest."

I wasn't sure how much of that was the girlfriend in me talking and how much of it was the industry expert, but the ring of truth from both sides was loud and clear.

"There will be some pretty upset fans, but I think you're right. It'll blow over relatively quickly and, hopefully, make the right impression with the guys who make the Blockbusters."

He was somewhere else, probably piecing together the press release he'd have to put out. Stepping away from the kind of reputation he had was never easy. I'd seen actors try and fail more times than I could count and I knew the toll it could take on a person. Most people have major issues with letting down a single person; he was being faced with letting down thousands.

I didn't envy him his position.

"I should call Ryan," he ran a hand down my back before finally sitting up, "he's been my manager for a decade now. He should be the first to know. Then I get to figure out how to tell my brothers."

"You need me to do anything?" I offered, "I'm pretty good at the moral support thing."

"Thanks, babe," he kissed the top of my head and helped me to my feet, "but I think I've got this part. Ryan and his team will handle most of the hard stuff. I just need to figure out how to break it to him gently that he's losing a multi-million dollar client so that he doesn't have a stroke."

"Does he have any contacts outside of porn? I mean, does he really *have* to lose you? A good manager can make or break you when it comes to this industry."

Porter shook his head, "I need it to be a clean break. If I'm really gonna get out of this, it's gotta be totally and completely."

"I don't think that's really possible, Porter. Your brothers are both still major players in the game and you can't just cut them out of your life because you're changing direction. I have to strongly recommend you keep Ryan on-board if he has connections you can use to get a role."

"Hmm," he pondered as he stepped into his jeans, "I guess I can talk to him about it. There's a lot hanging on how this conversation goes and the best assurance I have right now is a loose hope that he takes the news fairly well. I'm gonna head home and get the ball rolling. Let's do dinner tonight and I'll catch you up on it then."

"Okay," I wrapped my arms around his neck, pressing my bare chest to his before he could put his shirt on, "call me if you need anything."

He leaned down and kissed me, "I'll talk to you soon."

I walked him to the door as he slipped his shirt over his head and left without a backward glance.

It would be at least four hours before he finished his business, so I set about figuring out how to best use the time to keep myself from going crazy waiting.

As usual, my best available option was Becks and Mitch. Those two could take my mind off just about anything.

I shot off the text and began to clean up the wreckage Porter and I had left behind. Twenty minutes later had the distraction I very much needed.

"Where's Porter this evening?" Mitch asked after a cursory glance toward Porter's usual spot on the couch, "And what happened to the end table and lamp?"

"He's got some work stuff to take care of." I intentionally ignored the second half of his question.

"Wait, he went back to making porn? I thought he was on hiatus!"

165

The pure and unbridled pleasure that washed over Mitch's face at the idea of having more videos of my boyfriend to watch made it almost pleasant for me to crush his dreams.

"Nope. Sorry. Different kind of work."

"An audition?"

"No," he was prying, "that was earlier today."

"You're killing me here, Holly."

"And loving every minute of it, Mitchel."

"No Porter tonight?" Becks asked before she had even made it all the way through the door.

"I see where your loyalties lie," I rolled my eyes.

"Porter's off making porn," Mitch smiled over my shoulder at her.

"He is?" The joy on Becks' face was comparable to Mitch's.

"No. He's just taking care of some work stuff," I interjected.

"Work stuff is porn stuff where Porter's concerned," she countered. Becks was more hopeful for more naked Porter than Mitch had been.

"Not this time," I confirmed, "he's putting together a press release for his agent. He has some stuff coming up that needs to be addressed a little bit ahead of time."

"She's holding out on us, Becks," Mitch pouted as he returned with three glasses of wine, "I already tried. She won't give us anymore."

"Secrets don't make friends, Holly," Becks chided.

"You're already my friends, Rebecca. I'm not trying to make any new ones. Besides, loose lips sink ships and I'm not done with my cruise on the S.S. Porter. You can ask him yourself the next time you see him. If he doesn't mind telling you his business, he'll share. If not, you can hear about it with the rest of the world."

"Buzz kill," Mitch whined.

"You don't have a buzz to kill yet, drama queen."

He smiled at me and raised his glass, "Oooh! You're right! Let's fix that!"

"I'll drink to that!" Becks cried as she lifted her own glass.

"Amen, sisters," I touched my glass to theirs and we drank.

"Mmm," Becks swallowed her wine quickly, "Since you're not in a sharing mood, I guess I'll go first!"

Mitch and I both stared at her, waiting for her to share whatever it was she was practically vibrating over.

"Becks, I have wine to drink, spit it out."

"I landed a job today."

"What?" Mitch shrieked, "Honey, that's *fabulous*!"

"Becks! Why the hell didn't you say anything sooner? You let me sit here wallowing like a little bitch through half a glass of wine!"

"It's nothing major, but it's not a commercial or a shitty horror movie either! I'm pretty excited about it!"

Mitch and I set our glasses down on the coffee table and each of us claimed a shoulder. Becks laughed at us as we snuggled up to her in celebration.

"Even if it was a toothpaste commercial, we'd still be excited for you, babe!" I gushed. "I knew you'd make it happen!"

"Yeah," Mitch agreed, "as long as it wasn't like, a denture glue commercial or something. That would be a little too far below you. I don't think I could be proud of you for that."

"It's a supporting role in a film by a new director, but it's for a Lion's Gate film. This is my shot at the big leagues, guys!"

The sound of shattering glass ruined the moment and all three of us screamed like we were being shot at. When nothing else came crashing through the front of my house, we cautiously rose from the couch and went to peer through the hole in the window of my front door.

A huge rock sat below it in my entry way wrapped in a piece of tattered paper.

"What the fuck, Holly?" Becks asked, her hand shaking in mine.

"When did you move to the projects, girl? This is some bullshit!" Mitch's hand was also shaking.

I reached down with a trembling hand of my own and loosened the paper from the projectile that had just come through my front door.

Letters of different colors, fonts, and sizes had been cut out of magazines and newspapers and glued to the page like a ransom note from a bad movie.

"What does it say, Holly?" Mitch asked from his position at Becks' side.

I licked my lips before reading it for them, "Watch yourself slut."

"Fuck this! I'm calling the police!" Beck's marched up to my now-useless front door and yelled through the hole, "You hear me? I'm calling the police! I hope you enjoy jail you sick bastard!"

I sat down on the couch in shock, both unable and unwilling to believe what had just happened. It's not like I lived in Compton. I fished my phone out of my pocket and sent a text to Porter while Becks relayed what had happened to the police.

"You doing okay, Holly?" Mitch sat down beside me and briskly ran a hand over my knee, "Do you need anything? More wine? Some water? Food?"

"Wine," I agreed, "Thanks."

"Of course!"

He retrieved our glasses from the coffee table and hurried to the kitchen to fill them.

Two glasses later, I was beginning to feel a little bit better and my shock was slowly replaced by fury.

"Who the hell would do something like this to me?" I demanded of Becks, "I mean, I've had sex with *one* person in the last billion and a half years! That *hardly* makes me a slut, right?"

"Holly, if sleeping with one person makes you a slut, I don't even want to know what that makes Mitch." Holly laughed into her wine, "He must be the new whore of Babylon if that's the case!"

"Amen to that, sister!" Mitch raised his glass to her.

"Holly?" Porter's voice came from the front porch.

"In here!" I called back, "It's open! Obviously."

"What kind of city do we live in where your boyfriend can get here from across town faster than the police?" Becks scowled.

"Are you okay?" Porter hurried to where we were all piled on top of the couch and began a thorough search of my body for injuries.

Porter

"I'm fine, Porter," I smiled weakly, trying to push him away, "We were all sitting in here when it happened. None of us are hurt, just a little shaken up."

Mitch's hand shot into the air, "I think I might've been hit in the penis, Dr. Porter. I can't tell for sure though. I should probably be checked out!"

Porter raised an eyebrow at him and I playfully slapped his arm as Becks and I giggled at his sad attempt.

"You're a bottom, Mitch. You don't need a penis anyway. I think you'll be okay."

Porter's rebuttal sent Becks and I into fits of giggles.

Mitch didn't find it nearly as funny.

There was a firm knock at the front door followed by the tinkling of more falling glass as more shards were shaken loose.

"I'll get it," Porter rose and went to greet the police.

"Miss Nash?" one of the officers asked, glancing back and forth between Becks and me. I raised the hand holding my wine glass.

"That's me."

I stood to greet him as his partner came around the corner as well and extended a hand in greeting.

"I'm Officer Perry and this is my partner Officer Branson."

"Hello," I shook hands with Officer Branson as well, "thanks for coming."

"We just have a few questions for you before we get any deeper into the scene of the crime."

"Of course, let's have it."

"What time did it happen?"

"It was just a few minutes before we called it in."

"I placed the call at six twenty-two," Becks chimed in, "So we were attacked at about six eighteen."

Officer Perry looked to me for confirmation. "We weren't attacked, Becks," I nodded my head at the officer, "the time sounds about right though."

"Can you think of anyone who would want to hurt you, Miss Nash?"

"No!" I cried, "I mean, outside of some failed Hollywood wannabes who just never made the casting cut, I can't think of anyone who could possibly hold a grudge. And even then, do you really think someone would do *this* just because they couldn't land an audition?"

"We live in L.A., Miss Nash, you'd be surprised by some of the messed up stuff we see from jaded actors. Do you have a list of recent clients who bombed their auditions?"

"I do!" Mitch chimed in helpfully, "I can email it to you right now, or I can fax it in tomorrow when we get into the office."

Officer Perry tipped his head in Mitch's direction, silently instructing Officer Branson to take care of it.

He asked a few more basic questions, wrote down all of our contact information, gathered up the rock and the note, then left us to clean up the mess.

Mitch and I swept up the broken glass while Porter and Becks went to the store to find something to temporarily cover the gaping hole in my front door.

By the time the night wound down, we were all too tired to do anything about the food situation and all three of them refused to leave me alone in the house. Mitch and Becks each took a spare bedroom and Porter and I fell into my bed, exhausted.

"Who would do something like this to me?" I asked, annoyed when my voice shook.

"I don't know, Holly, but they'll find whoever it was."

I lifted my head so Porter could slide his arm under me and pull me close to his side.

Without the adrenaline to keep me going, my body began to tremble and my voice cracked, "Someone knows where I live, Porter, and they clearly have no qualms about causing physical damage to my home. What if that's not enough for them? What if they come after me next?"

Tears had welled up in my eyes and I was moments away from falling apart completely.

Porter turned his head and kissed my forehead, "I'll be here, Holly. I won't let that happen."

The first of many tears fell onto his chest.

Porter

"I'm scared, Porter."

He ran his hand up and down my back as I silently cried myself to sleep.

The last thing I remember was his soft whisper.

"So am I, babe. So am I."

Ninteen
Porter

After the incident with her front door, I practically moved into Holly's house full-time. I couldn't bring myself to leave her alone any longer than absolutely necessary. I moved half my wardrobe, all of my toiletries, and asked the front desk at my building to hold my mail for me.

I couldn't take the chance that something else would happen to her while I wasn't there. There was a part of me that still held onto the anger over letting it happen the first time and I didn't think I could handle any more self-loathing.

I didn't tell her this, but I felt somehow responsible for what had happened. If I had been there, I could've at least chased down the bastard who did it and beat the shit out of him until the police showed up. Then he'd be off the streets and my girlfriend wouldn't be terrified of her own shadow and anything that went bump, creak, or groan in the night.

For the first week, she'd hardly slept at all. The sound of the wind blowing outside would wake her up and then she'd sit there all night waiting for someone to come in and chop us up into tiny little pieces.

It got to the point that I'd strongly considered slipping her some sleep aids in her dinner. Nothing I said could comfort her on those nights and, worst of all, sex was off the table. I could barely even touch her without her flinching.

Luckily, things eventually settled down and I didn't have to drug my girlfriend to get her to sleep. We settled into a routine surprisingly fast and life continued to happen around us.

Porter

"You're going to be late for your meeting," I urged as I ushered her toward the door, "You should've been on the road ten minutes ago."

"Meet me for lunch today?" she asked as she slung her purse over her shoulder.

"I can't today, babe," I caught her and spun her into my chest, "I've got a lunch date with a porn star."

The flash of concern that sparked in her eyes told me that my joke had missed its mark.

"My brother, Holly," I clarified, "Parker asked me to meet up with him for lunch today. This reconnecting thing between us is still a bit touch-and-go. I don't want to cancel on him and risk fucking it up."

"Oh," I could see the wheels in her head turning as she chastised herself for letting it get to her, "Sorry, I'm a bit flustered lately. Tell Parker I say hello! I have to go. Busy day today! Let's do dinner tonight!"

"You got it!" I smiled at her and leaned in for a kiss, "And after dinner, can I have you for dessert?"

She laughed, "I'll have my people call your people and see if we can pencil it in."

I kissed her one more time and smacked her on the ass, "Get out of here! Speed safely! Oh! And my retirement goes public today!"

"Then tonight we celebrate!" she waved over her shoulder and closed the door behind her.

I moseyed around the house for most of the morning with a cup of coffee and the latest issue of *People*. I even made the bed and did a load of laundry before I got in the shower and headed out to meet Parker.

As I drove to the restaurant, I planned out a menu in my head for dinner that night. Holly wouldn't be expecting a home-cooked meal and it had been a while since I'd stretched my culinary legs.

I put the last item on a shopping list in my phone before getting out of the Land Rover and heading for the front door of the place Parker had picked to meet for our lunch.

David Michael

Once inside, I had no trouble spotting his table. It was the one with half a dozen women standing around it giggling.

Of the three of us, Parker was the one who most loved the spotlight. Preston and I were always more likely to lay low and avoid the attention when we were out just trying to be normal. Not Parker, wherever he went, he soaked up the attention like a sponge. It was like a drug to him.

It was a better option than coke though, so I never gave him shit for it.

"Excuse me ladies," I slid through Parker's harem and into the booth beside him, "I've got a lunch date with my little brother. Would you guys mind giving us some space?"

Seeing two of the Hale brothers in one place was a rarity outside of industry functions, so fans tended to get a bit excited about it when it happened. We agreed to a few pictures for the sake of getting them the hell away from our table and, after they left, Parker was all smiles from ear-to-ear.

"Six girls, six phone numbers, and all I had to do was sit down at a table," he bragged, "We've seriously got it made."

I laughed, "Parker, if you had sex on camera as often as you do *off* camera, *then* you'd have it made. You've gotta stop giving it out for free, man!"

"What can I say?" he grinned, "I've got the sex drive of a teenager and no short supply of easy targets. I can't help myself!"

"I worry about you, Parker," I shook my head and smiled, "I mean, think about it, how many kids do you have that you don't even know about?"

He screwed up his face and shook his head, "No way, bro. I'm always safe. You know how I feel about having kids. I'd be a terrible parent. Not a chance in hell, buddy."

I shrugged my shoulders, "You never know is all I'm saying. There are some shady bitches out there that would do some extreme shit for the chance to give birth to the next Hale. It's pretty much a golden ticket to the life most of these women can only dream about."

"Speaking of women," I could tell he didn't like the direction the conversation was heading in and let the change in topic slide for the time being, "How's Holly? You're pretty much living with her now, right?"

I nodded my head, "Yeah, pretty much. And she's great. Like, *really* great. I never saw myself as the domestic type before her, but there's just something about that woman that makes me want to jump every time she snaps her fingers. Not that she does that, but you get what I'm saying. She's independent to the point of driving me nuts, so every chance I get to help her with something, I'm all over it. Hell, I got mad at the window installers when they came to fix her front door. I half expected her to demand that they let her do it herself. When she didn't it was kind of a kick to the ego, ya know?"

"Oh my God, Porter," he was laughing at me and shaking his head, "You're in love with her!"

"What?" A feeling of panic reared up in my stomach, "I am not! It's only been a few months, Parker! Don't be stupid. I just want to help her out where I can. That's normal behavior for a boyfriend, isn't it?"

"Of course it is," he agreed, "but getting homicidal when someone else gets to do something for her is a little extreme, I think. Face it, Porter, she's got you by the balls."

"You're so full of shit. It's not like you would know love if it slapped you upside the head with a brick anyway."

"Oooh," he quirked an eyebrow, "Getting defensive about it now, are we?"

"I'm not defensive, I'm just saying I can't possibly be in love with her. You know how we Hale men work. Hell, I'm not even sure we're *capable* of actually being in love. Look at our parents! Dad wasn't exactly a gleaming example of how to treat the people you're supposed to care about. I'm not a family man, Parker; any more than you or Preston. We're just not wired for it."

He scoffed and shook his head, "That's bullshit and you know it. Mom and Dad had their issues, but you can't deny he loved her with every fiber of his being—In his own, demented, unconventional way—probably. At some point, I'm sure."

"Maybe," I glanced around for the waiter, praying for a valid excuse to derail this conversation, "The service here blows!"

"You're just mad that I'm right about something for once," he laughed as he waved his hand and nodded at a passing waiter, "Just because our dad fucked up his marriage doesn't mean we're doomed to the same fate, Porter. We're all better people than he was. Mom raised us to be better than him and, for the most part, she did a damn fine job of it." He turned to the waiter without missing a beat, "I'll just have water with a lemon."

"Same for me," I told him, "and a bottle of your darkest beer, please."

"You're a good man, Porter," he continued after the waiter walked away, "You were the father figure when we were kids, you're still the father figure now, and it's time for that to stop. We're all adults now. I have to accept responsibility for my actions, and Preston is more responsible than both of us put together. It's time for you to focus on *your* life. It's time for you to make yourself happy for once. Holly can help you do that if you'd just quit being a stubborn ass and let her."

I had nothing to say to him. My brain was completely blank.

"Are you guys ready to order?" the waiter asked as he set our drinks down in front of us.

"Give us just a minute," Parker said as he picked up his menu.

I followed suit even though I wasn't really hungry anymore.

"I really like their pastas here. I've never ordered the same thing twice and not once have I been disappointed. You could probably throw a dart at the menu and still get something delicious that you didn't even know you were in the mood for."

I followed his advice and picked something at random. We placed our orders when the waiter came back and something about the forced interaction kicked my brain back into gear.

"How's sobriety treating you?" I asked before taking a long sip of my water.

"It's good so far! I think I've got myself back under control. I don't *crave* it anymore. That was the hardest part, I think. You know how I am when it comes to being told I can't have something."

I laughed, "I think that's a genetic trait. The men in this family have always gotten what they wanted. It was bred into us."

"You'd think people would learn not to tell us no, right?"

There was a glimmer in his eye that I hadn't seen since we were kids. The part of me that had been in charge for the past fifteen years reared it's ugly head and pointed an ugly, shriveled finger at me.

You let that light die once. Don't do it again.

"I'm really glad you're off that stuff, Parker. It was killing you and there was nothing I could do to stop it. You're looking great and I'm willing to bet your bank account says thank you. What are your long-term plans? We haven't talked about it in a long time. I remember when you landed your first contract you were all about buying a house and getting your pilot's license so that you could buy a plane. Is that plan back on the table? Has the dream changed? Who are you now, Parker? I want to know my little brother again."

One side of his mouth was raised in a gentle smile as he recalled the glory days. We were all practically kids at the time and had the entire world at our feet. Anything had been possible for us.

"You know, I haven't really though much about it lately. Now that you mention it though, there's still a part of me that wants that. I've spent enough time living the party life and you're right, it almost killed me. I think it's probably about time I grow up and remember what was important when I was still myself."

"What can I do to help?" The prospect of Parker finally getting his shit together kindled something inside me that demanded I do everything in my power to help keep him on that path.

"I think you missed the whole point of the conversation we just had, Porter. It's not something you should have to help with. My life is something I'm responsible for, not you. You know as well as I do that I have the power to make this happen for myself. It's just a matter of applying some self-control, right?"

I nodded my head, "It's easier said than done, Parker. I've had my days where I just want to go out and blow all my money. I mean, I have enough of it, right? And there's always more to be made. But I don't want to find myself ninety years old and broke. Therefore, I exercise a little bit of restraint when it comes to living the lavish lifestyle I'm perfectly capable of pulling off. At least for the short term."

"You don't think I know a little something about restraint at this point?"

There was a smile on his face as he said it, so I knew it was more something he was proud of than him telling me I was being a dick.

"Sorry," I apologized anyway, "I guess I don't know how to turn off Big Brother Bot. You've managed to get clean without me, I'm sure you can manage to do whatever it is you want to do on your own, too. But just keep me in mind if you ever need help, or a co-pilot, or even just an older brother to bitch to when life doesn't treat you fair."

"I *do* miss having people to talk to," he smiled over the two plates of food between us as the waiter set them down, "I've kind of had to alienate myself from everyone I hung out with while I go through this. I think I'm getting back to the point where I can hang out with them again without getting crazy."

I didn't like the idea of him putting himself back in that situation, but I bit my tongue and didn't say anything. If I was ever going to get used to the idea of him being an adult, I needed to start practicing. If there was one way to test his self-control, a party with his old friends was it.

Besides, don't they say that relapse is a part of recovery? Addicts are allowed to make mistakes along the bumpy road to sobriety, right?

God, I hoped he didn't make that mistake.

"Enough heavy shit," he decreed, "I'm starving to death over here. Let's eat."

I smiled at him and tried to shut off the part of my brain that kept telling me to advise against him hanging out with his old friends.

We ate our meal in silence. Not because we had nothing to say or because we were uncomfortable, but because the food was delicious and I couldn't shovel it down my throat fast enough.

Porter

I washed the pasta down with the last swallow of my beer and sat back against the booth with a heavy sigh. It had been a long time since I'd stuffed myself so full of food that I had a hard time breathing and I quickly remembered why I didn't make it a habit.

"Holy shit," I groaned, "I think I'm gonna explode."

"I feel your pain," Parker rubbed his stomach with his palm, "I need to take a nap while this food baby incubates."

As soon as the word "nap" left his mouth, I could feel my eyes getting heavy. I couldn't afford a nap. I had a dinner to make. Napping was *not* an option.

"Let's get the hell out of here before I pass out on the table," he flagged down the waiter again and asked for the check.

Outside in the parking lot, we exchanged an awkward goodbye hug and headed for our cars.

"Be safe!" I yelled across the pavement.

He waved over his shoulder in acknowledgment and I had no choice but to consider it a success that he didn't flip me off.

I hit the grocery store on my way back to Holly's house and picked up all the stuff I'd need. I hauled it all into the house in one go and dumped all ten bags on the kitchen floor in a pile.

The need to pee had hit me halfway through the grocery store. By the time I stuck my key in the front door, my teeth had been close to floating out of my head. Groceries could be put away *after* I answered the call of nature.

I'm a firm believer in the theory of toilet gravity and that day was no different than any other: The closer I got to the toilet, the closer I got to pissing my pants.

My phone vibrated in my pocket and I quickly washed and dried my hands so I could check the message. It was a text from Holly letting me know that she'd be out of the office right at five o'clock. It'd take her half an hour to get home, giving me just under an hour to have dinner cooked, plated, and on the table. It'd be tight, but I could do it.

I was chopping like a mad man a few minutes later when my phone rang on the counter next to me. I answered on the first ring and hit the speaker button.

"Ryan," I answered as I grabbed an onion and continued chopping, "What's goin' on, man?"

"Well, Porter," I could hear the stress in his voice, "are you sitting down?"

"No, Ryan, I'm not sitting down. I'm trying to make dinner for my girlfriend. Why are you on my phone?"

"With you being a big actor now, I just didn't want you to faint and break your face or something. A fucked up nose and some black eyes isn't going to land you any roles, dude."

"Ryan, I'm fine," I set the knife down and splayed my palms on the counter, giving all my attention to my cell phone, "Spill it."

"Well, it's been an interesting ride, my friend. As of three hours ago, you're officially retired from the porn industry." He blew out a long breath, probably waiting for me to respond. I was busy trying to sort out the warring emotions I felt about his announcement though, so he kept talking, "The first few blogs went live as soon as I hit send on the email and they just kept trickling out there. Once the news hit social media, it went viral within an hour. From what I understand, most of the major news stations will be covering it on the five o'clock news here in a few minutes. I wanted to be the one to tell you so that you didn't have to hear it from the TV."

"You should've insisted that I sit down, Ryan," I found myself leaning heavily against the counter to keep myself from sliding down the wall and spending the rest of the evening sitting on the kitchen floor.

"I tried, Porter. You, as usual, didn't want to hear anything I had to say."

"You're not exactly known for dropping bombshells on me like this though. I wasn't expecting it is all. It's a bit of a shock."

"You sound like my bank account, Porter."

The line went dead and I was left with my silent phone, a pile of vegetables to be chopped, and steak fajitas to make for two.

The screen flashed to life with a buzz one more time, displaying the time and a message from Holly. Five o'clock on the dot.

Just leaving the office. See you soon!

Porter

"Shit!" I got back to chopping with a vengeance and tossed the strip steak into the frying pan. I doused it in olive oil and spices and waited for it to start sizzling. I didn't want the veggies to be soggy, so I had to wait until the meat was nearly done before adding the bell peppers and onions.

I sent off text messages to Parker, Preston, and my mom to tell them my retirement was official and poured myself a glass of wine. I flipped the meat in the pan and stepped around the corner to set up the bar with plates and a wine glass for Holly. I was down to ten minutes until she was due to walk in the door.

I added the veggies to the pan and prayed that everything would come together nicely in the end.

I tossed the tortillas in the microwave at the last minute and filled the wine glass I had set out for her.

Hot plates, silverware, and containers of food slid into place at five thirty-one and I stepped back to survey what I had put together for her. Something was still missing, but I couldn't quite put my finger on it. I glanced around the room hoping that something would trigger an idea.

"Candles!" I snapped my finger as the idea hit me and ran into the bedroom. I grabbed two of the tapers Holly kept on the windowsill but never lit and carried them back into the living room dining area.

Once they were burning brightly, I shut off all the lights, grabbed her glass of wine, and took up residence in the entryway to wait for her to get home.

I checked my phone compulsively for the next ten minutes.

No texts and no phone calls came through.

I finally broke down and hit the call button. It rang six times and went to voicemail.

"Holly, where are you, beautiful? Call me back."

I disconnected the call and placed her glass of wine back on the counter. I gathered up the rapidly cooling food and put it in the oven so that it would stay warm.

A text went out moments later saying the same thing my voicemail had and I began to pace. It wasn't like Holly to be late home without saying anything. We had a schedule and, until that point, neither of us had deviated from it without some kind of notification.

Something wasn't right.

I called her phone again and got the same reaction: Six rings and voicemail.

I pulled up Mitch's number and dialed.

"Porter?"

"Yeah," I felt like a total fuck tard calling him, "Hey, have you seen Holly?"

"Not since she walked past my desk at five o'clock. She was in a huge rush. Said she was meeting up with you."

"That was the plan, but she's not home yet."

"Wait," I could hear his confusion even over the phone, "You didn't pick her up?"

"No," I didn't like where the conversation was heading, "I had lunch with my brother and came straight home to start cooking dinner for her. She texted me on her way out of the office to let me know she was on her way, but I haven't heard from her since."

"Porter, her car was still in the parking lot when I left."

My stomach sank.

"Do you think Becks picked her up?"

"Maybe. Want me to call her and check?" I could hear the panic edging into his voice.

"Would you?"

"Of course!"

"Thanks, Mitch. Let me know as soon as you know anything?"

"You got it, handsome."

The line went dead and I cursed under my breath.

Pacing a hole in the floor was starting to seem like a pretty legitimate prospect. I laid out a track around the couch and began making laps. It was somewhere around the tenth lap that my phone rang.

"Tell me something good, Mitch."

"Becks hasn't heard from her either," he sounded more freaked out than I was, "I don't like this, Porter. Becks and I are on our way over. We'll set up a plan of attack and go from there."

Porter

The other line beeped through, "Gotta go, Mitch. The other line's ringing."

I hit the green button to answer the intruding call, "Hello?"

"Porter!" It was Becks, "I'm on my way over there. Have me a glass of wine ready and call me the *moment* you hear from her if she contacts you before I get there."

"I'd love to if you and Mitch would stop tying up my phone to tell me that you're on your way here."

"See you in three minutes," and the line went dead.

I continued to walk circles around the couch and didn't bother breaking my stride when Becks stormed through the door like a tornado.

"Wine me," she demanded.

"The glass on the counter is all yours."

Mitch was right behind her.

"I brought wine!" he announced, waving the bottles above his head like war banners.

"I called her phone six times on the way over here. I got voicemail every time," Becks told us, "She's never ignored me that many times in a row."

"I called her too," Mitch said, "Six rings and voice mail."

"Fuck!" I roared into the room for lack of anything better to say. Becks and Mitch both jumped at the sound of my voice.

"What the *fuck*, Porter?" Becks yelled, holding a hand to her chest, "Are you *trying* to kill us? You almost gave me a heart attack!"

"Holly is *missing*, Becks, and I can't do a fucking thing about it! I don't even know where to start looking and it's been an hour and a half since any of us have seen her. She could be fucking *anywhere* by now!"

"Have you called the police yet?" Mitch asked in an attempt to calm me.

"I thought about it on my way over here," Becks said, "but they won't start looking for her until she's been gone for at least twenty-four hours. She's an adult and won't be considered a missing person until then."

"What if she doesn't *have* twenty-four hours, Becks?" Mitch was beginning to fall apart right before my eyes and I needed to do something to rein us all back in.

I needed to give them something to do to keep them occupied.

"Let's start looking then. Someone should stay here in case she comes home. Maybe she lost her phone. Becks, think you can handle that?"

She nodded her agreement, "Wine will keep me company."

"Mitch, you start back at the office. Search every square inch of that property and find me *something* to work with. If she's missing, there's gotta be a clue as to where she went. People don't just vanish without a trace."

"I brought the wine, how come I don't get to stay at the house? Why do girls always get the easy jobs?"

Becks and I just stared at him until he agreed and stormed out the front door.

"What are you gonna do, Porter?"

Now that the question was there to be answered, I wasn't really sure.

Unfortunately, I didn't need to think very hard about it. My phone vibrated in my hand and I nearly dropped it in my haste to read the text that had come through.

It only took two sentences to bring my world crashing down around me: If you want to see her again, you'll be here by 7:30. 5873 Pierpont Ave.

I called the number that had sent the text as I ran out the door. It went straight to a generic voicemail.

"This had better be some kind of sick fucking joke you son-of-a-bitch or I'm gonna rip your balls off and stuff them down your throat until you choke on them!" I screamed into the phone.

Mitch had almost closed the door to his car when I flew down the steps and b-lined it for the driveway.

"Porter!" he yelled, "What's going on?"

"Get inside with Becks!" I yelled back as I climbed behind the wheel and threw my phone across the cab as my Land Rover roared to life and peeled out of my spot in Holly's driveway.

Porter

I had eighteen minutes to get all the way across Los Angeles County.

The world around me blurred as I slammed on the gas pedal and tore through the neighborhood.

Seven minutes.

Twenty

Holly

The stench of old motor oil and sawdust hung so heavily in the air that I had to fight the urge to gag. I knew I was close to the ocean because I could taste the salt, thick and briny on the air. It felt like there was a pillow pressed over my face though, so none of my senses were clear. It was all a massive, awful jumble.

Someone nearby was slurring and groaning. The pitiful sound echoed off distant walls and high ceilings, further disorienting my groggy brain.

Eyes, Holly. You have eyes. Use them.

I focused every iota of concentration I had into opening and focusing my abnormally useless eyes.

I felt them flutter open, my brain told me they were open, but I couldn't see anything.

Dammit, Holly. You've gone blind. You couldn't have picked a better time to lose the use of your eyes?

My eyes weren't the only things that had stopped operating properly. My arms and legs didn't seem to be communicating with my brain either.

Was I in a horrible car accident? Am I a half-deaf, fully blind, quadriplegic woman now? Wait, am I drooling?

A sharp slap across my cheek cleared some of the cotton in my brain and the brilliant bursts of color that erupted in the darkness forced me to question whether or not I had actually gone blind. The cogs in my head began to turn again, informing me that my arms and legs did in fact still have feeling in them. I could feel the rope that fastened me to the chair cutting into my wrists and ankles.

Porter

Hearing came next. It became painfully clear to me that the pathetic noises filling every inch of spare space in my head were coming from my own mouth. What's worse is the fact that I was uncontrollably begging some invisible assailant to let me go.

"You're not going anywhere," a quiet voice hissed in my ear. Those four words snaked around the inside of my skull like an electric train on a track. With each pass they grew louder until they became a dull roar that nearly drowned out the sharp click of receding steps.

All at once, my senses came into sharp focus and my brain finally received the messages my extremities were sending it.

I was tied to a chair, blindfolded, covered in bruises, and I had, in fact, been drooling on myself. Waves of nausea rolled through my stomach and sharp jabs of pain tore through my entire body.

I peeled my sandpaper-dry tongue off the roof of my mouth and formed what sounded to me like a complete sentence. In reality, it was a bunch of indistinct slurring with one clear word thrown in for good measure: "Why?"

"*That,*" my captor screeched, "is the million dollar question, isn't it?"

The clear sound of stilettos clipping back in my direction added a spark of terror to the agony I felt in every inch of my being.

My head was ripped backwards by my hair and before I could scream, something was stuffed in my mouth and tied in place.

"You don't get to speak to me you fucking slut!" Another slap across the face punctuated the tantrum, effectively driving her message into my brain like a railroad spike.

"In brighter news," her voice went from psychotic to almost amicable, "he hasn't shown up yet which proves my point that he really doesn't care if you cease to exist. Conveniently enough for me, I would *really* like to see you not exist anymore. My only hurdle now is deciding how to make that happen. I think I'll give him a little more time while I make up my mind. There needs to be some kind of incentive that will both encourage him to show up *and* keep me entertained enough to keep you alive. He needs to see the end of you. For the sake of motivation on all sides of this triangle, I have informed him that for every five minutes he's late, I will be breaking one of your fingers. If I run out of fingers, you run out of time. Oh look, four minutes have gone by already. Which finger would you like me to start with?"

I tried to plead with her through the cloth gag in my mouth as she ran a single, slender finger down each of mine. It was like a twisted game of This Little Piggy.

"Let's start small," she whispered. Her mouth was so close to my ear I could feel her breath as it brushed over my cheek.

She pried the pinky finger of my right hand out of its balled position and held it wrapped in her palm for a moment, "This is probably going to hurt."

I could hear the cruel smile in her voice as she said the words and I screamed as loud as my hoarse voice would allow. She stood there, my pinky in her hand, silent, until I stopped wailing and broke down into sobs.

Then there was a sudden pressure accompanied by a gut-wrenching crack as she violently shoved my pinky flat against the back of my hand.

I might've screamed, but the cotton had returned to my brain. I was sure I had tipped over in my chair from the world listing so sharply to the side, but I never felt myself hit the floor.

I continued to sob as my body worked through the shock and my pinky began to throb.

"For some reason," she began to pace around my chair, "I thought you'd be stronger than this. I'm disappointed in how little fight there was in you. I expected thrashing and swearing and yelling, but all you've done is mumble and whine and beg. You don't deserve him. You know it, I know it, and he knows it. That's why he's not here. He's probably happy I'm taking you off his hands. I'm not sure what he *thought* he saw in you but clearly, the illusion has been broken. Now Ryder can get back to his normal life—the life that didn't have you in it. The life he made with me."

Who the fuck is this crazy bitch?

My brain kicked into survival mode and I tried to think of ways to keep her talking without actually engaging her in conversation. The only thing I could think to do without the ability to speak was to struggle. I had to put up the fight she wanted and keep her from getting bored.

I tried to rock the chair side-to-side and back and forth. I pulled against the restraints holding me in place as hard as my exhausted limbs would allow, but nothing budged. In the end, I was only able to violently shake my head and scream against the gag in my mouth.

It wasn't much, but it seemed to do the trick.

"That's more like it," she leered, "still a pretty pitiful display, but at least it's *something*!" A tiny electronic beep went off somewhere in the room and she clicked her tongue, "Another five minutes down and still no Ryder. Shall we just go in order?"

She pried the ring finger out of my weakly balled fist and without waiting for me to stop fighting, slammed it backward until my fingernail touched my wrist.

The larger bones filled the air with a louder crack than my pinky had and sent an immediate blaze of pain up my entire arm. I screamed until my voice gave out and tried, against my better judgment, to lash out at her with my feet. I'm pretty sure I lost consciousness at some point. However, when the agony of my middle finger being snapped five minutes later wracked my body, I was most definitely awake.

She had my thumb gripped firmly in her hand when a door somewhere in the distance slammed. We both froze. I even held my breath, straining my ears in hopes of hearing something, *anything*, that would tell me my savior had come.

The silence hung in the air between us like darkness, deep and seemingly impenetrable. I didn't need someone to drop a pin to tell me how quiet it was, I could hear the bitch's heart pounding in her chest.

The longest ten seconds of my life passed in this manner before the best sound in the world finally rang through the space as clear as a bell.

"Holly?"

It was Porter's voice.

He had finally come for me.

David Michael

Twenty-One
Porter

"Holly?" I yelled into the shadows of the massive warehouse. My voice echoed loudly off the walls as I strained my ears for any kind of response.

I thought I heard a muffled voice, but by the time my own voice had faded it was gone.

"Holly, babe," I shouted, "If you can hear me, I need you to make some noise! I can't see anything in here! Tell me where you are, sweetheart!"

The loud hum of industrial lighting filled the air as a single bulb against the far wall blazed to life. I could make out two figures—one was slumped over in a chair, and the other was standing beside the first holding its hand.

My feet pounded against the concrete before I even realized I was moving.

When I was close enough to make them both out clearly, my heart stopped as I skidded to a halt.

Holly was bound to the chair, limp and bleeding from the corner of her mouth and nose. I could see the sickly yellow of a fresh bruise forming beneath the blindfold over her eyes. Duct tape held her wrists, ankles, and shoulders to a heavy steel chair that had been bolted to the floor. Four of the fingers on her right hand were bent at grotesque angles and her thumb was captured in the palm of a finely manicured grip.

"Vanessa?"

"Hello, Ryder."

Porter

My brain struggled to comprehend what I was seeing. I looked back and forth from one woman to the other, trying to make sense of it all.

"We've been waiting for you," Vanessa announced happily, "We can finally put an end to all of this madness now! You don't have to retire anymore! I've taken care of it! You can come back to me and we can go back to the way things were!"

Vanessa jerked Holly's thumb backward and dropped her hand like it was an empty hamburger wrapper. The weak yelp of pain that came out of Holly shot straight through me, shredding my heart like razor blades through paper.

"What the *fuck* Vanessa?"

I moved to help Holly, but before I could take two steps Vanessa had reached behind her and pulled out a handgun. She pointed it at Holly's head.

Okay... So too much coffee can *make aerobics instructors snap. Good to know.*

I froze and put my hands in front of me.

"Woah," I placated, "Vanessa, what are you doing? This is *crazy*!"

"It's not fucking crazy!" she screeched frantically, "You need this, Ryder! We had a life! *You* had a life! Then *this* bitch came along and tore it all apart! You're blinded by her, Ryder! You can't see what she's done to you! We had *everything*!"

"Vanessa," I pleaded, "what the hell are you talking about?"

"Before you met this *whore*," she spat the last word like venom, "you were the leader of an *empire*, Ryder. The world was yours. We were happy together! We made love! I invited you into my home, into my bed, and you made me believe I was your queen! She took that away from us, Ryder!"

The gun in her hand trembled with fury. I needed to get her away from Holly before she could do anything stupid. I took a single, careful step forward.

Vanessa pressed the barrel of the pistol into Holly's temple, causing her head to loll to one side under the pressure. A quiet whimper escaped through the gag in her mouth and I knew then that I would do *anything* to save her.

"Vanessa, come on, baby," my brain was going a million miles an hour trying to figure out how I'd get us both out of this alive, "We can still have that! You know me. Nothing can stop me from getting what I want. I can make it happen for us, V. Put the gun down. Let's talk about this."

"Don't fucking placate me!" she shrieked, slamming the butt of the pistol down on Holly's forearm, "I saw the press release today, Ryder! You're retiring! You're throwing your life away for this little home-wrecking slut! I can't let her take your life away from you! I won't! The only way I can stop her and break whatever hold her cunt has over you is to end her and we both know that! I wanted you to be here for it! I want to see you realize what she had done to you! I want to see your face when you realize that what we had is exactly what you need. You need someone who will support you and encourage you and love you for who you are, Ryder! Not someone who strips away your dreams and forces you to give up the life you've worked so hard to build for yourself!"

"Vanessa! For fuck's sake! She didn't force me to give up anything! I still have everything I want! I've wanted to get out of the porn industry *almost* since the first day I got into it! It was a stepping-stone for me the whole time! I never meant to make it a life-long career! Do you understand that? I don't want to be a glorified prostitute for the rest of my life! It's *always* been my plan to retire early and chase my dreams in another direction! You want to be a part of that, don't you?"

"Of course I do," the fury in her face gave way to something more gentle, but equally psychotic, "but *she* took that away from me."

"Vanessa," I reached a hand out toward her, "Put the gun down and come with me. Let's get out of here. Thanks to you, I can see what she did to my life. You broke her spell on my and saved us. She's powerless now. Leave her. Let's go."

The bitch had *clearly* snapped and my only hope was to play into her delusion and make her believe that she had already won. If I could get her close enough that I could get the gun away from her, I could knock her out or break her wrist or give in to the urge to rip her throat out with my bare hands.

Porter

I choked down the terror that threatened to burst out of me like water from a broken damn and managed to hold my outreached hand steady.

She stared at the limb like it was her salvation, a gentle smile softening the madness into an almost-pathetic sense of longing.

"I can't," the hardness returned to her face as she snapped back to the present, "We can't leave her here to be found alive. It's too risky, Ryder. She could find us again and ruin everything. I can't live like that. I can't live with the constant fear that she might take it all away from me again. She has to die."

A single shot rang out in the darkness.

Time froze right along with the beating of my heart.

Twenty-Two
Holly

The sound of dozens of heavy footsteps was the only thing that told me I wasn't dead. I was physically and emotionally numb and barely felt the cool brush of sharpened steel against my flesh as my arms were cut free.

Someone jerked the blindfold off my head and the harsh, overhead light blinded me. Everything was fuzzy as half a dozen black figures moved around me in slow motion. The world slowly rocked back and forth making me feel seasick.

I tried to make out Porter's voice in the rumble of the crowd, but someone flipped a light switch somewhere in the distance and flooded the entire world with a brilliant, burning glow. The pain shot into my skull like a hot poker just before everyone vanished and everything went black.

When I finally came to my brain was foggy once more, but the lights were low and it didn't hurt to open my eyes. There were strange, quiet noises and the room was unfamiliar, but when my eyes fell on Porter, none of it mattered anymore.

"Hey," I tried to say. It came out as more of a croak, but it was enough to get his attention.

He jumped to his feet and took the two steps from his chair to my side, tenderly brushing his hand over my forehead. "Hey," he crooned, "How you feeling?"

"Thirsty," I rasped.

"The doctor said you might be," he gently slid a spoonful of ice chips into my mouth, "He thinks you were chloroformed and one of the side effects is severe dry mouth."

Porter

I sucked on the frozen water and relished the soothing, hydrating sensation as it melted and slid down my throat.

"What happened?" I asked when the ice had finally moistened my throat enough that I could talk without feeling like I was breathing sandpaper.

Porter slid another scoop of ice between my lips before he pulled the recliner over to my bedside and gently took my left hand in his, "You were kidnapped and held in a warehouse for a few hours. Your car was still parked outside your office, so they think she grabbed you on your way out." His eyes misted and I could hear the tears strangling his voice, "I'm so sorry, Holly. I never meant for this to happen."

"Not your fault," talking was still difficult and there was a dull pain creeping into my right arm, "Who?"

"It *was* my fault though. The woman who took you was a crazy fan and someone I'd met a few times. She taught Jazzercise at my gym. If it hadn't been for me, she wouldn't have even known who you were. When she saw the press release announcing my retirement, she snapped. Apparently, she'd been following us for weeks. The police say it was her who threw the rock through your window. They found a stack of magazines with letters cut out of them in her car and photos of us all over her apartment. She'd been obsessing about it since our second date. I'm so, *so* sorry, Holly."

I cringed as a new wave of pain washed through my arm.

"She broke all the fingers on your right hand and fractured your ulna," he pressed the button to call the nurse, "It's probably about time for another dose of pain killers."

I squeezed his hand with what strength I had and tried to smile at him. I could see the worry and the guilt etched on his face as clear as day. He was beating himself up over it and looked like he hadn't slept in days.

"How long?" I asked.

He blew out a heavy breath as the first tears spilled over his eyelashes and traced wet trails down his cheeks, "She had you for just over three hours. You've been in the hospital now for two days. After they put everything back where it belongs, they kept you pretty heavily sedated. You've been barely conscious for the last forty-eight hours."

Two days? How was that even possible?

"Becks?"

"I called her and Mitch when you didn't come home that night. They met us here after everything went down and the three of us have been taking shifts at your bedside. They're down in the cafeteria getting coffee and food right now." His tears were flowing in full force at that point, "It's all my fault that this happened to you. I'm so sorry."

He bent his head to my hand and pressed his lips to my fingers, sprinkling me with the warm tears still falling from his eyes.

"You rescued me, Porter," I freed my hand and placed it on his cheek, "You saved my life."

"If it wasn't for me, you wouldn't have needed rescuing in the first place."

"Porter," frustration had strengthened my voice, "I love you. I would do it all again for you in a heartbeat. It took the prospect of not being able to tell you for me to accept it, but it's true. I love you."

His mouth hung open and he stared at me like I had just done some kind of magic trick.

The nurse chose that moment to come through the door and smiled at me warmly when she realized I was lucid.

"Is that arm bothering you?" she asked as she checked the bags near my head and adjusted a few unseen knobs.

"A little bit but it's tolerable."

"Well, that's the joy of modern medicine. You don't even need to tolerate pain anymore," she flipped through the chart at the foot of my bed and made a quick note, "I've gone ahead and given you another dose of painkillers. Give it a couple of minutes to kick in and just give us a call when you're ready to eat."

"Thanks," I said with a half-assed smile.

She nodded curtly and smiled before leaving the room to continue her rounds.

Porter

The delicate brush of Porter's thumb over my hand drew my attention back to him.

"I love you, too, Holly. I'm sorry it took almost losing you for me to tell you. Even Parker and Preston tried to tell me, but I just couldn't see it. It wasn't until I saw you in that warehouse, bound and broken, that I knew I would do *anything* to keep you safe. Never in my life have I ever considered myself capable of killing someone but, given the chance, I would have snapped her neck, Holly. I would kill for you. I'd die for you, Holly Nash. Do you understand that?"

I smiled at him as my head began to swim from the drugs pumping into my veins through the IV in my arm.

"I do, Porter. I really do." I had to fight to keep my eyes open, "Don't leave me. I think I'm falling asleep."

"You're stuck with me, Holly. I'm not going anywhere."

I felt the soft press of his lips to the back of my hand once more.

The last thing I heard before I gave into the pull of the medication was a whispered promise; "I'll keep you safe as long as there's breath in my body."

Epilogue
Porter

After two more days in the hospital, Holly was finally allowed to go home. Becks and Mitch had packed up all of her stuff and all the get-well flowers and cards that had covered every inch of every flat surface in her room. They were walking behind us, chattering on as usual while I pushed Holly down the hall in the wheelchair the hospital insisted we use.

I leaned down and kissed the top of her head, "You excited to be out of here?"

"You have no idea," she replied dryly, "Mostly, I just want to take a bath and eat a cheeseburger. Being trapped in that bed for four days was almost worse than the four hours in the warehouse."

I laughed quietly and sped up just a touch. She'd feel better with some sunshine on her skin and some fresh air. Being stuck inside had made her surly.

My phone rang in my pocket as I helped Mitch and Becks load the last of the flowers into the back of my Land Rover. It was my mom's ring tone, so I let it go to voicemail. I'd call her back after I got Holly home and settled in.

It started ringing again almost as soon as it had stopped.

"Sorry, guys. I gotta take this. It's my mom."

"I think the gay boy can manage to get some flowers into the backseat, Porter," Mitch joked.

"And I'll get Holly settled into the front seat," Becks assured me, "as long as that means I get to be the first to sign her cast when we get home!"

I nodded my thanks to both of them as I brought the phone to my ear.

"Who died, Ma? I'm trying to get Holly home."

"It's Parker," she was sobbing into the receiver and my breath caught in my lungs, "He's overdosed. He was partying with some friends early this morning and they all thought he fell asleep. The police won't tell me anything more than that."

I stood in the middle of the parking lot in shock listening to her cry on the other end of the line.

"Is he alive?" I whispered.

"I'm sorry honey," she said through gasping breaths, "I couldn't hear you."

"Is he alive?" I asked again, almost yelling the words into the phone.

"He's in an ambulance right now on the way to L.A. General."

"I'm already in the parking lot," an ambulance came tearing around the corner and up to the entrance to the Emergency Room, "They just pulled in, Ma. I'll see you when you get here."

"Get her home!" I tossed my keys to Becks and ran back toward the hospital.

I had a feeling I was about to witness the downfall of the Dick Dynasty.

David Michael

About the Author

David Michael is the author of The United Series - a five-book paranormal romance series - and the Dick Dynasty Trilogy.

His passion for writing was born of his passion for reading. He spent his childhood escaping into the worlds created for him by authors and has always aspired to join their ranks. After the publication of his first novel, he couldn't be stopped.

David lives in Salt Lake City, hates the snow, loves his pets and, more often than not, can be found sitting in front of his laptop in his underwear hammering away at the keyboard. He's a firm believer that what you put out into the universe comes right back to you and *always* looks for the silver lining around the rain clouds in life.

Connect With David

author.david.michael@gmail.com
www.authordavidmichael.com
www.facebook.com/authordavidmichael
Twitter: @Author_DM

Made in the USA
Charleston, SC
07 January 2017